"Let's talk about sex."

Giles turned to India, and she tensed visibly. "Wh-what do you mean?"

"Isn't that where your doubts creep in?" he queried, and India sucked in a distraught breath. "How did I know?" he asked, reading her thoughts. "You were so astonished, so uncertain afterward, as if it had never happened to you before, almost guilty. So I gathered it had been very different for you."

"I can't talk about it," India said at last.

"I don't want to pry into my father's love life," he said levelly. "But that might be one reason you were determined to write yourself off as a lonely widow ready to fall into the arms of the first man who came along—leaving aside the irony that they happened to be *my* arms."

LINDSAY ARMSTRONG married an accountant from New Zealand and settled down—if you can call it that—in Australia. A coast-to-coast camping trip later, they moved to a six-hundred-acre mixed-grain property, which they eventually abandoned to the mice and leeches and black flies. Then, after a winning career at the track with an untried trotter, purchased "mainly because he had blue eyes," they opted for a more conventional family life with their five children in Brisbane, where Lindsay now writes.

Books by Lindsay Armstrong

HARLEQUIN PRESENTS

559—MELT A FROZEN HEART
607—ENTER MY JUNGLE
806—SAVED FROM SIN
871—FINDING OUT
887—LOVE ME NOT
927—AN ELUSIVE MISTRESS

HARLEQUIN ROMANCE

2443—SPITFIRE
2497—MY DEAR INNOCENT
2582—PERHAPS LOVE
2653—DON'T CALL IT LOVE
2785—SOME SAY LOVE

These books may be available at your local bookseller.

Don't miss any of our special offers. Write to us at the following address for information on our newest releases.

Harlequin Reader Service
901 Fuhrmann Blvd., P.O. Box 1397, Buffalo, NY 14240
Canadian address: P.O. Box 603,
Fort Erie, Ont. L2A 5X3

LINDSAY ARMSTRONG

surrender, my heart

Harlequin Books

TORONTO • NEW YORK • LONDON
AMSTERDAM • PARIS • SYDNEY • HAMBURG
STOCKHOLM • ATHENS • TOKYO • MILAN

Harlequin Presents first edition February 1986
ISBN 0-373-10951-2

Original hardcover edition published in 1986
by Mills & Boon Limited

CHAPTER ONE

IT was a sparkling morning. The sunlight glinted on the leaves of young trees, the pavements were clean and the air smelt delicious after the rain of the night before. Only a block away the Pacific Ocean stretched a pale, morning blue to the horizon and the famous beaches of Surfers' Paradise lay golden in the sunlight.

India Ballantyne turned the corner that skirted Oskar's Garden Restaurant and paused a bit further on to gaze into the windows of one of the exclusive boutiques for which Orchid Avenue was becoming renowned. If you had the money, this end of the avenue was a shopper's paradise. If you didn't, it was still a delight to gaze through the elegant shop-front windows and you could always have a cup of coffee at one of the pavement cafés and pretend that you did.

India intended to do more. She had a favourite pavement restaurant which served bacon and eggs just as she liked them and she quite frequently breakfasted there, with the result that she was well known and as she sat down the waiter hailed her and came over immediately. 'You're looking very smart this morning, Mrs Ballantyne!'

'Thank you, Aldo,' she replied.

'Business?' Aldo enquired, as he spruced up the table.

'Business,' India agreed ruefully.

'Such a shame on a nice day like this! What would you like? The usual?'

'Yes thanks. How's your mother?'

'A very lot better, Mrs Ballantyne. Soon she will be back to work. She was very thrilled with your flowers!'

'Oh, I'm glad,' India said with a wide smile. Because she was a regular customer, she had come to know all the members of Aldo's family—new Australians who by dint of sheer hard work and dogged determination, now had this rather profitable little business going for them. India had often marvelled at how they worked together as a team and a family.

As she waited for her orange juice, she thought about this again and then with a pang, contemplated what lay ahead of her this sunny morning—a meeting of the board of the company of which she was a director. Fortunately these meetings only occurred quarterly ... otherwise I'd be a nervous wreck full time instead of only every three months, she mused, and sighed. And as she always did before board meetings, she fell to wondering if she at least looked the part while knowing that however conservatively and expensively she dressed, there was no way she could really look the part.

She looked down at herself in the latest of the series of outfits she'd worn over the past two years to board meetings, and wondered if she should have chosen another colour. Last time, she'd gone in a severely tailored navy-blue suit but it had been winter. And now it was spring and a lovely little two-piece, short-sleeved outfit in a clear, primrose yellow had captured her imagination so she'd bought it, teamed it with pale grey accessories and ever since, even while she'd been dressing in it earlier, been worried that it had been the wrong choice. It wasn't that it was frilly or anything like that. But it did seem to be—well, very feminine, she thought, as she fingered the polyester crepe of the gathered skirt. The jacket had padded shoulders with pleats running into the bodice and a fitted waist around which a wide, grey suede belt that matched her beautifully elegant, imported shoes and purse, sat. She wore several very fine gold chains of different lengths about the collarless neckline, another delicate chain with one gold charm on her watch wrist and on that hand her magnificent emerald and diamond engagement ring together with her gold wedding band.

Perhaps it is the colour, she mused, and smiled as Aldo presented her with her orange juice.

'Bacon and eggs coming up!' he assured her.

Half an hour later, she'd regretfully finished her breakfast, had one cup of coffee, and knew it was time to make a move. She always walked to board meetings. It seemed to help. But as a last-minute gathering of her defences, she opened her purse and pulled out her mirror, a tissue and lipstick and carefully redid her mouth. Aldo had supplied a hot towelette.

It was an almost perfectly oval face that stared back at her, with smooth, very lightly tanned skin—she didn't believe in sunbathing so her tan was more like a golden bloom that didn't hide the fresh colour in her cheeks. Her hair was as she more or less always wore it, parted in the middle and smooth about the parting, then loose in a cloud of dark curls to just above her shoulders. It was the kind of hairstyle that looked as if it might have cost a fortune to create; indeed it did for most people, but India had naturally curly hair.

But it was her eyes she was really inspecting. Her eyes that were brown with little green flecks in them, those eyes that were usually such a dead giveaway. Do they look anxious and nervous? she pondered. As I *feel*? Surely by now—after all I'm twenty-five—surely by now I've learned to mask my eyes?

'Oh, Mrs Ballantyne—how are you? You do look lovely!'

'Thank you, Fiona,' India murmured. Fiona Hardcastle had manned the reception desk of Ballantyne Enterprises for as long as she could remember, and had accepted India's metamorphosis from lowly typist to wife of the Managing Director with perfect poise—a thing others had found hard to do. Consequently, India had a soft spot for Fiona and always stopped to chat with her.

This morning, however, Fiona appeared a little flustered. 'I'm afraid the meeting has had to be put back half an hour, Mrs Ballantyne. Mr Kidder has been unavoidably delayed. And Mr Ballantyne would like to see you in his office.'

India's heart sank. 'Now?' she queried.

'As soon as you came in, he said.' Fiona lowered her voice a fraction. 'I think it's something to do with this new resort project. The island in the Whitsundays?'

India blinked. Ballantyne Enterprises was a company that developed holiday resorts, but she hadn't heard of this new project, nor, for that matter, had any intimation that they were prospecting so far afield from the Gold and Sunshine coasts where they were heavily involved. Still, she thought with a shrug, I suppose that's not so surprising—that I haven't heard.

'Why,' she licked her lips, 'would he want to speak to me about it?' she asked Fiona.

'I gather there's to be a bit of a fight about it. Some members of the board are against the idea.' As soon as she'd said it, Fiona looked briefly uneasy for she was normally the soul of discretion. Then she shrugged and thought, why should the poor kid be totally in the dark? She still thought of India as that despite the transformation India had gone through from those days when she'd been as poor as a church mouse, totally uncertain of herself—but so lovely even then.

She spoke then in a rapid undertone, 'Kidder and Ramsey are against it. Mr Ballantyne and Jeff Whitby are for it. You—will have the casting vote.'

India paled and thought, I knew this would happen one day! Oh God . . .

She swallowed. 'Why . . . hasn't anyone let me know?'

'It's all blown up almost overnight. Um . . . it might be an idea not to keep Mr Ballantyne waiting. He—isn't in a very good mood.'

India closed her eyes then took a deep breath and unconsciously straightened her spine. 'All right,' she said calmly.

But as she stood for a moment outside the door marked *Managing Director*, she was feeling less than calm, she had to acknowledge, and it took several more deep breaths to accomplish the little act of merely knocking on the door.

'Come in ...' The words were clipped and decisive and the tone unmistakably irritated.

India steeled herself. Then she went in and closed the door quietly behind her, and said, 'Good morning, Giles. I ... it's a beautiful day.'

The man behind the large desk turned a strangely contemptuous grey gaze upon her and Giles Ballantyne replied without rising, 'Morning, India. Yes, it is a beautiful day—so sorry you have to waste it in this manner.'

The contempt was in his voice too, and India gritted her teeth, but it seemed he hadn't finished. 'Do sit down,' he said lazily. 'You're looking gorgeous as usual, my dear.' He eyed her with detached interest. 'How much did that little outfit cost?' he added sardonically.

'It's got nothing to do with you,' she said tightly, and sat down with anger visible in the taut, straight line of her back.

'Well, in the sense that it was my money that bought it, I disagree with you. But as always, I can't dispute your taste.'

India controlled a sudden furious impulse to pick up the heavy paperweight on his desk and hurl it at him. She'd had those impulses before and learnt that they only left her feeling humiliated. Instead, she said abruptly. 'Why did you want to see me?'

He raised one eyebrow. 'Not rising to the bait today?' he queried idly.

'If,' India said steadily, 'you wanted to see me about voting with you for the island project, you're going about it in a peculiar manner, Giles, you really are.'

His eyes narrowed. 'How did you know about it?' he asked in a hard voice.

India felt a spurt of panic. She knew enough to know that Fiona's little indiscretion wouldn't be taken kindly to. 'I . . . I have my sources,' she said finally, in a surprisingly even voice.

'So they've been lobbying you already,' Giles Ballantyne said softly. 'Quicker off the mark than I thought. Was it Kidder? He always did look forward to the prospect of going to bed with you . . .'

India's hazel eyes flashed furiously. But she looked down immediately, her lips tight.

'Or Ramsey? For that matter he too isn't entirely unmoved by you and your *young* body, I suspect.'

India raised her eyes at last and Giles Ballantyne burst out laughing. 'Talk about—if looks could kill,' he said finally, and added, 'never mind, India, it doesn't matter one way or the other to me how you came to know about this, although we did have a little arrangement, I believe, that the name of Ballantyne wasn't going to be dragged through the mud; now, didn't we?'

She refused to reply and he watched her for a little while, her tilted chin and hate-filled eyes.

Then he stood up and came round the desk towards her and by some mighty effort of will, she forcibly restrained herself from shrinking back into her chair. For it could honestly be said that Giles Ballantyne, aged thirty-three, frightened the life out of her. And not only because he could always beat her in a game of words, but because of the latent strength and sheer masculine vitality of his finely muscled, taut, big body. He was tall—a good head taller than India, who was tall herself, for a girl. And there was a freedom about the way he moved that indicated someone very fit, and in a physical sense, more than a match for her.

She didn't know why she was so conscious of this with Giles and had pondered it from time to time because, in a physical sense, most men were more than a match for most women. Nor, since he'd never used any physical violence with her, did she have any basis for this particular fear she felt of him. But it was there and when you added the powerful, arrogantly intelligent force of his personality—well, she'd often been reduced to feeling as puny as a piece of paper in his company.

Which was one of the reasons she'd come to hate him so, and although she hadn't actually shrunk from him, there was a wary light in her eyes now as well. But he only sat down on the corner of his desk, about a foot away from her, and studied her contemplatively for a time.

Oh, well, India thought with a sudden surge of defiance, two can play at this cat and mouse game. And she stared back deliberately. At his thick tawny hair, his unusually dark grey eyes, at his unhandsome face which all the same was wildly attractive to most women, she knew. At his long square-tipped hands, his beautiful grey suit and dazzlingly white shirt . . .

'Cat got your tongue, India?' he said softly, but with a gleam of amusement in his eyes.

She flushed but said, 'No. It's just that I refuse to discuss anything with you, Giles, that isn't of a business nature.'

'This is.'

'Then let's get on with it. But I must warn you, any further insults and I'll simply walk out of here.'

He smiled slightly. 'Very well, India,' he mocked, mimicking her businesslike tones. 'I'll tell you what I wanted to see you about. At this morning's board meeting an issue will come up to the vote.' His eyes were suddenly hard and completely businesslike. 'And I thought it might be timely to remind you of the ... arrangement *we* have, you and I. That you vote with me on any issue. That the ... Ballantyne family sticks together. It is a condition we agreed upon, if you remember—of you maintaining your position on the board, receiving a director's fee, keeping your parcel of shares, your unit—in other words, your key to maintaining yourself in the manner to which you have become accustomed.'

India closed her eyes. 'You're so sure you could take all that away from me, aren't you, Giles?'

'If I were so minded, yes I am,' he said flatly.

'I could fight you every step of the way. The law ...'

'I should imagine you, my dear India, would be about as naïve about the processes of the law as anyone could be.'

'I could get a good lawyer.'

'If you vote against me this morning, India, you'll find yourself needing one. So,' he stood up, 'what's it to be?'

Occasionally India surprised herself. This turned out to be one of those occasions. She stood up unhurriedly and smoothed her skirt. 'You'll just have to wait and see, won't you?' she said sweetly, and walked past him to the door, which opened just as she got to it after a brief tap on it, to reveal Fiona's face.

'Er ... sorry to interrupt, Mr Ballantyne—Mrs

Ballantyne, but Mr Kidder has arrived and everyone else is assembled in the boardroom.

'Thank you, Fiona,' India said, and shot a triumphant glance over her shoulder at Giles Ballantyne.

The panelled board-room was high on the Nerang River side of the building that sat on the northbound lanes of the Pacific Highway. From its windows, that didn't open because of the air-conditioning, one had a commanding view of the Gold Coast hinterland however.

India stared out at the mountains, purple today in the clear air and wished herself up at Binna Burra, a mountain resort though not a Ballantyne's resort . . .

'. . . we are in the business of upmarket resorts,' Jeff Whitby was saying intently, 'and what we visualise, Giles and I, is a very upmarket one in the Whitsundays . . .' Jeff was an accountant by profession and an intense man who India in fact liked, which was more than she could say for the rest of the board. Possibly, because he was the only one apart from Giles who didn't, from time to time, let her know that he wouldn't mind her gracing his bed.

Giles *is* right about Ramsey and Kidder, she thought, and sent an intense look of dislike from beneath her lashes at Giles Ballantyne. They're always trying to touch me, and I can't help knowing that's one reason why I'm still on this board. But to think I would actually encourage it . . .

She glanced at the other two men. Lance Kidder was in his early forties, a forceful, good-looking and dynamic man and very able business-wise.

But, to India anyway, he literally exuded the air that he considered himself irresistible to women. It was a curious thing, she'd often thought, how some men did this in a mostly unspoken way, and how thoroughly unpleasant it was. Yet he had a devoted wife and two children. Also a rather jealous wife, India had realised on the odd social occasions she'd attended and been the recipient of some death-ray-like glances from Mrs Kidder. If only she knew how safe her husband was from me! she'd mused.

As for George Ramsey, he was a widower and sometimes rather sweet, she thought, but he must be sixty if he's a day ... Her lashes flew up and she put a hand to her mouth.

'Something bothering you, India?' Giles drawled.

'No. I'm ... interested, that's all,' she managed to say, and flinched inwardly at how lame she'd sounded.

'Go on then, Jeff,' Giles said impatiently.

'If I may interrupt,' Lance Kidder put in smoothly, 'the Whitsundays could be said to be in danger of becoming saturated, resort-wise. Hamilton Island, so I'm told, will eventually cater for several thousand people when it's finished. Then there are the resorts on Daydream, Hayman, South Molle, Lindeman, et cetera, plus the considerable tourist development at Airlie Beach on the mainland. Does it not occur to you, Giles, that we might have missed the boat?'

'Not at all,' Giles Ballantyne replied, and sat forward. 'Because nothing you've mentioned approaches the kind of resort I have in mind. The epitome of luxury, modern yet ...'

'At least Hamilton and Hayman could be considered luxury resorts and Hamilton is, at the moment, brand spanking new!'

'Ah, but the difference would be that I visualise the kind of place that would cater for fifty people at the most, a truly exclusive tropical hideaway—a millionaires' retreat,' Giles said.

'You mean—something like Lizard Island?' India said unexpectedly, then bit her lip because she'd spent her honeymoon on Lizard Island, several hundred miles north of the Whitsundays.

Giles Ballantyne turned his dark grey, sardonic gaze upon her. 'Something like,' he agreed drily.

'Another thing is,' Jeff said, 'with the airstrip on Hamilton now which takes jets, the Whitsundays are in a sense wide open. All it would take is a short helicopter trip to this island—or a boat. I believe Ansett is phasing out its Sikorsky flights from Hamilton to Hayman in favour of a new boat that's been commissioned to be not only a fast and very comfortable form of transport, but to act as a reception area, so that all the formalities of booking in are accomplished before you set foot on the island.'

'Well, it all sounds very appealing,' George Ramsey said then but cautiously. 'However, I never like to be rushed into things.'

'The lease is up for grabs,' Giles said tersely. 'It could be years before we get another opportunity like this. Nor am I, for one, rushing into things. I've done extensive feasibility studies and, for that matter, so had my father before me. I think you must all be aware that it was one of his dreams to have a Ballantyne resort in the Whitsundays . . .'

India closed her eyes, because she knew Giles would be looking straight at her.

'That's true, it was,' George Ramsey said. 'But we couldn't go into this on our own. We'd need subsidiaries and finance. Your father . . .'

'George,' Giles Ballantyne cut in, 'I don't claim to be the man my father was,' his mouth twisted, 'but have I let you down yet on the matter of subsidiaries or finance?'

'It's only been . . .'

'It's all in hand, George, as you'd see if you bothered to read the paperwork. And even if we did come to grief over finance, which we won't,' Giles said with a hard certainty, 'but even if we did, the lease is a marketable asset.'

'I'm sorry, Giles,' George said slowly, 'maybe I'm an old stick-in-the-mud, but . . .' He shrugged.

'Then we put it to the vote.'

'I doubt if it's necessary to go to all that trouble,' Lance Kidder said ironically, and India could tell that he was annoyed. He confirmed it by turning to her and saying with a barely concealed sort of insolence, 'Up until now we haven't had a major disagreement on this board. But it was bound to occur. India, I believe you have the casting vote on this occasion. How do you speak?'

India experienced a curiously liquid sensation at the pit of her stomach, and swallowed as all eyes rested on her. 'I,' she said in a low voice, 'am well aware that it was my late husband's dream to have a resort in the Whitsundays.' She looked up and straight at Giles. And well aware, she said but to herself, that that was your final lever, Giles. 'So I'm . . . for the resort. I think it's a good idea . . .'

There was silence for a moment. Then Giles

Ballantyne said mockingly, 'Thank you, dear step-mama. It's good to see that the family is ... united.' He smiled, but it didn't reach his eyes.

'Giles,' Lance Kidder said tightly, 'this is a ridiculous situation, you do realise that, don't you?'

'Then you should never have let my father appoint her to the board, Lance,' Giles replied softly. 'But you went along with him. In fact you all did,' he said contemptuously. 'I was the only dissenter on *that* occasion. You all let him jockey you and manoeuvre you into voting for her, despite the fact that you knew he was a ... besotted *old* man. And why? I'll tell you that too. Because you all visualised the day when he'd be gone and you fancied having a—soft, pliable girl on the board you could manipulate yourselves!'

'Giles!' George Ramsey looked shocked and distressed.

'I did nothing of the kind,' Jeff Whitby said evenly. 'I thought there was a lot of sense in your father's ideas on the subject, Giles. Mrs Ballantyne has excellent taste and very good ideas. I still think,' he looked directly at India, 'it's a pity you no longer play an active role in that area, Mrs Ballantyne.' He then turned a challenging look upon Giles.

There was a tense, horrible little pause. India was battling a desire to shed some hot, angry tears.

'All right,' Giles said into the nerve-racking silence. 'If that's what you think, Jeff, and perhaps I was a bit hard on you, she shall have her chance. I'm going up to spend a week on Hamilton—I want to have a good look at it now that Stage Two is finished, and one at our island again. You can

come with me, India, and give me the benefit of
your really good ideas. I'm getting an architect
and a surveyor out as well. What say you to that,
Mrs Ballantye?' he queried.

India stood up and discovered that her desire to
cry had quite left her. 'I would no more dream of
going anywhere with *you*,' she said through her
teeth, 'than I'd dream of consorting with a . . . a
snake! Why don't you take one of the glamorous
ladies you get photographed with so frequently?
Why don't you take six? Who knows, you might
wring an idea or two out of them,' she said
contemptuously and added coolly, 'good day to
you, gentlemen.' And stalked out.

Giles Ballantyne started to laugh ironically.

CHAPTER TWO

INDIA wrapped herself in her towel and sat hunched over with her arms around her knees, trickling sand through her fingers.

In a spirit of furious distaste, rage and God knows what else, she'd rushed home after leaving the board meeting, flung off her clothes, donned her swimsuit and beach things, descended fourteen floors in the lift from her unit, crossed the road and plunged into the Pacific Ocean as if it were a ritual, cleansing bath.

She'd swum for nearly an hour—not exactly swum but been in the water, body-surfing in on the smaller waves, diving beneath the bigger ones as Roderick Ballantyne had taught her to, and lying in the shallows with the silvery foam of the surf lapping her body.

She took a shuddering breath now and reached for her hat. Why do I let Giles get to me so? she mused. I *know* his father really loved me, *I* know the truth of how it all happened and that it was through no connivance on my part and not with any eye to inheriting *anything*, or taking his father for a ride ... or any of the other horrible things he's said about me. Is it because I'm a coward that I'm so ... vulnerable to all his taunts? So totally unable to handle this nightmare situation? Is it?

A tear dropped on to the towel where it covered her knees. I am vulnerable, she thought. I always was—Mum used to say that and worry about it.

20

You need to toughen up, India! Life knocks people like you around because you're so easy to hurt and you worry so much. Just take it one day at a time . . .

India sighed and laid her cheek on her knees and thought about her mother. Leila Lawson had been a rebel, of that there could be no doubt. She'd lived her young adult life through the sixties—a good time to be a rebel, she'd often said. It was really trendy then . . . Not that she'd been precisely a hippy or a flower-child, but she'd practised her own freedom of spirit, as she'd called it, in her own inimitable manner. Barely out of school, she'd set out to travel round the world, working her way as she went and doing it the way it should be done—poor, or so she'd thought. *How else can you really get to know people unless you have to work with them, live with them, as one of them?* she'd asked.

Several years later she'd come back to her home town, Melbourne, become very heavily involved in the Anti-Vietnam War campaign, and fallen desperately in love with a married man. The fact that he was married hadn't stopped them sleeping together but Lcila had perceived gradually the torment her lover was going through, torn between his wife and family, and her. And known that it could never work. She'd disappeared out of his life, more sorrowful than she'd thought she was capable of being, but none the less, resolute. She'd also been pregnant but had not told the father of her child . . . When the baby was born, her suffering had intensified once more, for the little girl gave evidence, even in those first few hours, of being very like her father. But Leila had got herself together again, and she'd named the child after the country she'd loved and spiritually felt most at home in.

India knew all this because her mother had been completely candid with her on the subject. 'I know it wasn't fair to you, or to him,' she'd said to India, when she'd thought she was old enough to understand, 'and perhaps you'll hate me for it one day, but—well, these things happen.' She'd gone on to explain how very complicated it would make India's father's life if it were discovered he had an illegitimate daughter.

'Would he hate me?' India had asked.

'No, not that.' Her mother's eyes had reflected an inner pain then, and a curious uncertainty—as if those clear-cut sentiments she'd once been possessed of were no longer that. It had been the only time she'd allowed the fact that she now questioned the wisdom of her actions to surface.

But India had not hated her mother for these revelations. In fact, for as long as she could remember she'd adored this lovely, vital person who had been the very centre of her existence.

And that had been what had seen her through a very unconventional childhood. For Leila Lawson had been true to her free spirit to the end. She had alienated all her relations, taken up a career as a singer—Joan Baez style until that had gone out of vogue—and carted India the length and breadth of the continent.

She'd often said to her, 'It's just the two of us, kid, on the road again!'

Yet India hadn't inherited her mother's self-confidence either, and the continual changing of schools, sometimes missing out on them altogether, the never-ending series of boarding houses and rented flats, had taken its toll too. Oddly, though, she'd always tried to hide the worst of her insecurities from her mother, as if it were a form of disloyalty.

The the unbelievable had happened. Although still lithe and attractive for her mid-forties, Leila Lawson had given away her singing career but not quite stilled the restlessness of her soul. She'd tried her hand at a variety of jobs in a variety of cities. Then she'd treated them both to a weekend at Surfers' Paradise, met a man on the beach who'd recognised her and offered her a two-year contract to sell real estate for him.

Leila had hesitated, glanced at India's expectant, breathless expression, and had heard herself saying yes . . .

They'd taken a twelve months' lease on a flat, the longest they'd ever taken, India had manfully struggled through her last year at school at yet another school, and never been so happy. It was the first taste of permanence she'd ever had.

She'd been older than the average school-leaving age when she'd set out to get her job with a mediocre Senior Certificate. It hadn't been much, that first job, and the company had folded after six months. But the next one had been much better—a typist with Ballantyne Enterprises, a very solid company in anyone's estimation, and with lovely offices in the heart of Surfers' Paradise.

India was about nineteen and a half when she'd been with Ballantyne's for one month. In fact, one month to the day after she'd joined them had been the day her world had come crashing down. Her mother had died in a car crash . . .

The police had arrived with the news while India was out to lunch, and it had been Roderick Ballantyne's unenviable task to break the news to her. That had been the first time she'd touched his heart.

She'd sat so still, her face white, her eyes heartbroken. And she'd seemed so helpless and utterly hopeless. Then she'd thanked him in a queer, stiff little voice and left his office. He'd picked up his phone and instructed Fiona to be on stand-by.

It was to Fiona that India had finally broken down and sobbed out the story of her life and the more heart-rending aspects of this tragedy. 'She was really happy at last, I think. And *settled*. We'd even moved to a new flat, a nicer one and unfurnished, and we bought our own stuff—we'd never before had that. Now . . .'

Fiona Hardcastle had relayed all this to her boss, Roderick Ballantyne because, not unaturally, he'd been concerned about India as one of his employees.

And any progress India had made over the last year or so, in the matter of self-confidence, seemed to have been destroyed. She was competent at her job but so quiet and reserved it was like working with a shadow, Fiona had once mused.

Unfortunately India had been struggling financially too. She'd had to move to a smaller flat because she couldn't afford the rent on a two-bedroomed one on her own, and she'd been left with the hire-purchase payments on some of the new furniture not yet paid for. In fact she'd been forced to take on a second job of waitressing three nights a week, to survive.

But the day had finally come when the furniture

had been paid off and she'd treated herself to breakfast in Orchid Avenue as a small celebration. Of all the lonely things she did, having breakfast at home by herself seemed to be the loneliest.

Roderick Ballantyne had been strolling down the avenue that Sunday morning, on his way to buy a paper, when he'd seen India..

He'd hesitated, suddenly disturbingly conscious that he thought a lot more about this virtual lowliest of his employees, than he should. And that he'd taken to watching her whenever the opportunity presented itself, but with the utmost discretion. The fact remained, however, that India touched something within him as a man as well as evoking a strongly protective instinct. For one thing she was unusually lovely in a totally unassuming way; for another, he knew of her financial struggles again via Fiona who'd only prised it out of India one day when she'd looked so tired. Fiona had been really worried and demanded to be told why. And Roderick had racked his brains to come up with some way of helping that wouldn't be misinterpreted.

She'd also appealed to his sense of style because although she dressed very quietly and cheaply, he'd guessed, there was an instinctive taste about it.

All in all, he realised that sunny Sunday morning as he watched India eating her breakfast, she delighted him, made him feel young despite the fact that he was more than old enough to be her father ... Am I falling in love? he had wondered with a sense of incredulity.

And he crossed the avenue to find out.

Three months later they'd been married.

*   *   *

The realisation that Roderick Ballantyne was in love with her had come slowly to India. At first she'd worried about the fact that the Managing Director, not to mention the man who had built up Ballantyne Enterprises, should want to see her outside office hours, for a variety of reasons. What people would think, what he really wanted from her were some of them. But, curiously, she'd never been uncomfortably conscious that he was so much older than she was. In fact she'd had no idea how old he was and was considerably surprised to find that he was forty-nine—a great age when you're not quite twenty. But he hadn't looked old, apart from his sprinkling of grey hairs. His body ws fit and tanned and hard, and he had the energy of someone much younger.

Then, after going out with him a couple of times because she hadn't known how to say no without offending him and she wondered if it mightn't affect her job, she'd discovered that she really enjoyed his company. She had no idea how this had come about, she had been nervous enough to stunt any potential friendship. Yet he had the knack of being able to make her relax. And gradually, in spite of her worries, she discovered that she liked nothing so much as being in his company. Too shy to ever feel at ease with the more forward approach of the boys her own age who had tried, from time to time, to date her, her personality responded like a flower to the sunlight, to his handling of her. He treated her like an adult and a friend and the things they did together, like going to the beach or the movies, or driving up to the hills for a picnic, gradually won her confidence.

Then the day had come when he'd put his arm

around her and kissed her gently on the lips. She hadn't responded but she hadn't broken free either, only stared up at him with her eyes widening, in sudden acknowledgement that she understood how he felt.

And she'd thought confusedly that she'd never before felt so safe as she did at that moment, standing close to him with his arm still around her.

When he asked her to marry him, Roderick insisted on pointing out the pitfalls of it from her point of view. 'I'm so much older than you,' he'd said, 'it will be something we'll have to decide whether it's wise to have children. And you mustn't forget that when you're . . . thirty, say, I'll be sixty, an old man. On the other hand I'll be able to provide you with security and—love. I love you, India, as I don't think I've ever loved.' And he'd told her about his first marriage which had been an unhappy one, and his son Giles who'd been overseas ever since India had joined Ballantyne's.

'. . . The only thing he didn't warn me about,' India Ballantyne murmured to herself, coming out of her reverie on the same beach they'd swum together from so many times, that day of the disastrous board meeting, 'was how his son Giles was going to hate me from the moment he laid eyes on me at our wedding reception.'

She shivered as she remembered.

They'd been married privately then held a small reception in Rod's unit. Giles Ballantyne had returned from America where he'd been studying the resort business, that same day just in time for the reception. Whether he'd been summoned home by his father India had never known. But she'd had no difficulty, as she stood there in her pretty

white voile dress with a garland of tiny white
flowers in her hair, in deciphering as she looked up
into those dark grey eyes for the first time, the
look of shock in their depths. Or the look of anger
that had flared briefly before being deliberately
doused.

Nor had she ever been able to forget what he'd
said to her by way of greeting, with a smile on his
lips and too low for anyone else to hear.

'Well, you've found yourself a nice sugar-daddy,
haven't you, love? I'm Giles Ballantyne, by the
way, your new ... stepson, I guess.'

Her lips had parted and her eyes been stunned
and she'd looked round instinctively for Rod, but
something had taunted her in those dark grey eyes
when she'd looked back in confusion, and she'd
known that for Rod's sake, the best thing she could
do was ignore Giles Ballantyne's dislike of her.

It had become a game from then on between
them, her and Giles. A cruel game. Of course Rod
had been aware of his son's disapproval of his
young bride, but never, thanks to India, known of
the barbed comments or caustic remarks Giles had
addressed to her from time to time.

It had also dawned on India for the first time, at
her wedding reception, that some people might
imagine she'd married Rod Ballantyne for his
money.

They'd had four years together. Four wonderful
years which neither Giles nor anyone else had been
able to sully. Years during which India had felt
she'd grown another dimension. The lack of
insecurity and worry had seen her bloom, and
during that time she learned so much from Rod
Ballantyne; they read together, travelled together,

and he encouraged her to develop talents which for the most part had lain dormant within her.

In the process of encouraging her to talk about her childhood, he unearthed two significant things—that she liked to paint but was quite sure she was no good at it. And that she was fascinated by architecture—not so much the mechanics of building, but designs and decorations and the character and styles of buildings.

From then on, he bought books on the subject and wherever they went, they discussed what they liked and what they didn't. They even began to draw up plans for their dream house . . .

Rod also had the spare bedroom of the unit converted to a studio for her and been less surprised than India had at the quality of her painting. And it had become an absorbing hobby for her.

Then he came up with the suggestion that she work part time for Ballantyne's in an advisory capacity.

'As an advisor?' Her hazel eyes were wide with surprise. 'What about?'

'Don't look so shocked!' He grinned at her. 'Come over here and let me explain.'

She went to sit on the floor at his feet as she so often did, and he ran his hand through her hair and told her about a new resort that was on the drawing-boards and how he thought they could use some fresh ideas on design and style which he believed she could supply. She'd just redecorated the unit, and he'd been so pleased with it that he'd said that they could probably use her suggestions for the interiors.

India protested that she wasn't qualified for that

kind of thing. But Rod overruled her. 'Put it this way, what I'm looking for, and what I think you could supply, is not a set of concrete specifications about anything. It's your ideas I'm interested in . . . your vision of things, your sense of style. Good ideas are as important as the technical stuff.'

Everyone apart from Giles had agreed that India's ideas were good, very good. He had said nothing. He'd had plenty to say, though, when Rod had had India elected to the board of Ballantyne's; but his father had ignored it. By then, anyway, the rift between them had been so wide that it had only been one more dispute in a long line.

Rod had only ever talked to her once about Giles, to say sadly that his son had been the product of a desperately bitter and unhappy marriage, and that he could understand why Giles, on occasions, seemed thoroughly to dislike both his parents. And India had known that although they fought, Rod Ballantyne loved his only son, which was why she'd gone out of her way never to let him know how much Giles hated her.

Then, not quite as out of the blue as it had happened with her mother, but in the matter of a few short months, Rod had been taken ill with a fatal disease and had died with her name on his lips. And her world had come crashing down again.

But to make matters worse, when she was still stricken with grief and feeling more alone in the world than ever, Giles Ballantyne had arranged a meeting with her in his office, and in a harsh voice and with hard, burning eyes, had told her that he considered she had no right to any of the things his father had left her and that he felt he had every right to contest the will.

What the legacy had amounted to was the housing unit, a parcel of shares in Ballantyne's and an interest-bearing investment that would yield her an income for some considerable time. In other words she'd been left well off, but Giles had inherited the bulk of his father's estate.

India had blinked at him and then it was as if every contemptuous thing he'd ever said to her, all his torments she'd suffered silently had risen up within her and she'd acted totally un-characteristically. She'd flung herself at him, beating at him with her fists at the same time, crying that he was only jealous because his father had loved her more than him . . .

It had been a terrible thing to say, and in fact it hadn't occurred to her until about a split second before she'd uttered the words. But she'd known immediately she'd struck home, as his face had whitened with fury. She'd stopped dead, hating herself a little.

Only to find herself hating him even more not many minutes later for what he'd said then. Because none of his veiled remarks of the past four years had come close to anything like this.

'If you contest the will,' she'd said, as white as he was when he finally finished, 'I'll fight you every step of the way.'

'You'll end up destitute, India,' he warned. 'Not only that, but your name will be a household word and your so-called love for my father will be turned inside out. His name will be bandied about too, but I don't suppose you care about that?'

She took a breath.

'Think about it, sweet stepmama,' he drawled.

She realised she wasn't quite understanding things. 'Have you ... come here to bargain with me?' she whispered. 'Do you want me to ... give it all up willingly?'

'Would you?'

She was unable to answer.

He laughed then. 'No, I thought not. And no, I had something else in mind. You see, what my father had not anticipated was the fact that he would leave behind him two rather clearly demarcated factions on the board of Ballantyne's: myself and Jeff Whitby on one side and Lance Kidder and George Ramsey on the other side. Now I've been appointed Managing Director, but I know Kidder would love to step into my father's shoes, and I know that Ramsey supports him. He thinks I'm too young and rash, possibly. But I intend to maintain my position and I have the numbers—that is with you voting with me always, I do, India.'

She stared at him blankly.

'Don't you see what I'm getting at?' he said impatiently.

'You won't contest the will if I . . .'

'Precisely. If you undertake to support me all the time on the board. You see, dear stepmama— and I don't for the life of me know whether my father intended it to be this way—you are now in the position of having the casting vote.'

India closed her eyes as that sank in.

'You've come a long way in four years, haven't you, India?' he said ruthlessly.

She opened her eyes. 'Rod couldn't have intended it to be like this. He didn't expect to die so soon, for one thing. He . . .' He loved you, he would never have set me up in a position to be one up on *you*, she wanted to say but she knew, looking into Giles's hard eyes, that it would like banging her head against a brick wall.

And all of a sudden, she was assailed by a curious feeling of guilt. I came between them, she thought, but I wasn't to know. And I don't think he'll ever understand that it was the last thing I intended . . . oh God!

'All right,' she agreed dully. 'I will vote with you.'

He didn't look surprised, only sardonic. And he said, 'One other thing; we'll maintain the fiction that you married my father for love for a decent period, India. In other words,' he went on softly, 'you will not—console yourself with any other men until a proper period of mourning has passed.'

'It was no fiction!'

'Then prove it,' he said curtly, and left.

India sighed heavily and realised she was cold, even wrapped in her towel. She also realised she'd spent a good part of the afternoon wrapped in her morbid reminiscences, and she collected up her things and headed for home.

She showered, grimacing at the fact that she was a little burnt on her shoulders and back; she'd applied sun screen to her face before plunging into the water but had neglected her body. So she put on a cool, silky caftan in a soft jade green colour with nothing underneath it, brushed her hair until it shone and left her face as it was with only an application of moisturiser. Then she poured herself

a glass of pineapple juice, put on one of her
favourite records and sat down in the lounge
opposite the glass doors that led to the terrace so
that she could watch the sunset.

But because it had only been a little over a
year and because of her tormented wanderings
down memory lane, she looked around the
room, and could feel Rod's presence as if he
were there.

Because they so rarely entertained at home,
when India redecorated the unit she had done it
with just the two of them in mind, so that the
lounge had only one settee covered in brown
velvet. By way of company it had an antique wing-
back chair adjacent to it, unusual in that it was
mostly wooden like a monk's chair but with a
padded seat and backrest upholstered in turquoise
silk with birds and strange-looking griffins woven
into the silk in pinks and violets. An Abbot's
chair, she'd often thought, and Rod had often sat
in it to think, he'd said.

Between the chair and the settee was a square
table set cornerwise with a heavy glass top and
solid, tubular brass legs. It bore only two items, a
tall lamp with a dusky pink, raw silk shade and a
straight heavy-bottomed crystal vase crammed
with fresh violets.

The wall-to-wall carpeting matched the turquoise of the chair and on one wall there was a
built-in bookcase with a beautifully carved frame,
and on another a long cabinet that housed,
concealed from view if necessary, a television,
stereo set and a cocktail section. Above the cabinet
was a large, gold-framed oil painting of a clump of
ghost gums in a sandy setting—one of India's, and

illuminated at night by an Italian cut-glass lamp that threw its light softly upwards.

The whole area was uncluttered and spacious— too spacious nowadays, India thought miserably, and laid her head along the back of the settee. And worse, it reminded her so much of Rod! Why did she stay? Wouldn't she be better to put this all behind her, to go away and start a new life? Now that her paintings were selling, she had some money of her own—she didn't suppose it would ever be a fortune, but they were doing much better than she ever dreamed they could. And surely that would be better than all the tortures she was going through at the moment? Of not being able to forget—not that she ever wanted to forget Rod, but the pain of being without him was ... *And I could resign from the board.*

She turned her head into the crook of her arm and forced herself to examine her curious reluctance to do just that. Was it because she was afraid that the next person they elect would side with Kidder and Ramsey? Is that why she submitted herself to anything Giles did? Because she felt *guilty* about his being in the position he was in? I shouldn't, she thought, I really shouldn't, but the fact is I do feel responsible in some strange way, for the fact that the rift between Rod and Giles widened so much.

She sighed and lifted her head and stared unseeingly out at the last rays of the sun, with sudden tears streaming silently down her face.

She heard the doorbell ring once but ignored it. Then when it rang again imperatively, she ineffectually scrubbed at her face and went listlessly to answer it.

It was Giles Ballantyne.

CHAPTER THREE

THEY stared at each other in silence for a moment. He was still wearing the grey suit he'd had on at the board meeting and there were lines of weariness beside his mouth. But his eyes were, for once, impossible to read as they scanned her briefly from head to toe, and came back to rest on the tearstains still visible on her face.

'India,' he said quietly at last.

But she came to life. 'No,' she breathed distraughtly, and tried to slam the door, 'this is one place where I don't have to put up with you!'

'I want to talk to you . . .'

'Go away!' she panted, still trying to close the door on him.

'Don't be a fool, India,' he said sharply, and somehow got them both inside and closed the door with one hand while he held her wrist still with the other. 'I've come to . . . call a truce,' he said to her wide and suddenly frightened eyes. 'Please hear me out.' But the tone of his voice was clipped and curt.

'I don't believe you,' she whispered, and wrenched her wrist free. 'Anyway,' she added in a stronger voice, 'it's too late for a truce! Nor am I interested in one. I hate you!'

'All the same, you will hear me out,' he said dispassionately. 'And I'd prefer not to have to forcibly make you do it.'

The threat was implicit and she backed away a step involuntarily, which caused him to say impatiently, 'For God's sake, India, let's behave like adults!'

'You ... oh!' She almost choked on her rage, which brought a gleam of amusement to his eyes.

'The civilised thing to do actually, would be to invite me in and offer me a drink—I've had a hell of a day,' he murmured with his lips quirking. Then his eyes narrowed and he added in quite a different tone, 'You haven't had an easy one for that matter, have you, India?'

She would have given anything to be able to retort acidly that no, thanks to him, she hadn't! Instead she found she could only look at him in silent screaming frustration and despair. And worse, with tears threatening again.

She took a breath. 'All right,' she said tonelessly. 'One drink while you say what you came to say, but don't count on it changing anything. What will it be?' she asked over her shoulder as she led the way into the lounge.

'Scotch and water, thanks.'

He stood in the middle of the room looking round while she poured his drink and a glass of sherry for herself.

She handed his glass to him and sat down in the Abbot's chair because she couldn't bear to think of him sitting there where Rod had sat.

'You've changed this place,' he commented idly.

'Yes.'

'Since . . .?'

'No. About two years ago.'

He lifted his eyebrows. 'I didn't realise it was so long since I came here last.'

'It's longer,' she said flatly, 'but let's not go into that. What did you come to say to me?'

He loosened his tie irritably. 'India—I want you to come to Hamilton Island with me. No, let me explain . . .'

'You don't have to explain anything,' she said through stiff lips. 'It's the last thing I'd do. Why?' she asked suddenly, intently. 'Is it going to affect your position on the board if I don't? I don't see how it possibly could, but that's about the only reason I can imagine you having.'

'It's got nothing to do with the board.'

'Then why? You must have a reason. You can't expect me to believe it's for the pleasure of my company!'

He looked down at his drink. 'Put it this way. I think it's time we . . . stopped warring with each other, and this would be a good way to do it. I also think Jeff's right, you do have a certain—feel for things. I only have to look around here to know that. It's beautiful. And it's very important that we get this resort right. That's why I'd like to have your advice on styles of architecture and so on, which you couldn't give unless you'd seen the island.'

'Giles,' she tilted her head to look at him, 'I tried to tell your father this, believe me, but I'm not trained for this kind of thing. You're talking about the kind of expertise that would cost you a fortune to get normally, whereas all I have is,' she shrugged, 'beginner's luck, probably, if that. Besides which, I'd be petrified to do it. Don't you see?'

'I'm not asking you to take any responsibility— all I'm asking is that if it . . . kindles any ideas, you let us have them. Is that so unreasonable? You'd have done it for my father—you would still be doing it for him in a sense. Ballantyne's was his creation. It meant a great deal to him.'

'Do you think I don't know that?' she whispered.

'Then will you come?'

'No.'

He swore beneath his breath. 'Will you tell me why, then?'

'I should have thought it would be obvious. Over the last five years you've repeatedly humiliated me, made it perfectly clear what you think of my morals, made my life a misery over the last twelve months and it wasn't that happy to start with . . .'

'I've only seen you four times in the last twelve months, India.'

'That was enough,' she retorted bitterly. 'But what really amazes me is the fact that you seem to think you can call *all* the shots. You can start the war and then think you can say all right, let's call it a day, and imagine that I'll go along meekly with it! You must be mad if you think that! Only this morning you treated the board to a scathing denunciation of your own father and therefore me, indirectly—I'm only surprised you didn't go the whole hog and say some of the things to them you've said to me in private over the years, I'm really surprised . . .' Her voice had risen gradually and although she was dimly aware that hysteria was claiming her, she couldn't do a thing to stop it and began to cry jerkily and laugh at the same time.

He regarded her silently, then put his glass down abruptly, and pulled her to her feet and held her in his arms.

'No! No . . .' she wept and struggled feebly.

Giles said nothing, just held her to him with an easy strength that she'd always known he possessed, until she was too exhausted to struggle any more. But it was an age before she stopped crying and then she could only lean against him— Giles Ballantyne of all people—weakly.

He picked her up and sat her down in the corner of the settee and swung her legs up on to it, then sat down beside her. 'Look,' he said quietly, 'you're right. I have treated you abominably. And you were right about the reason. I *was* jealous. Because in all the years of growing up, I was plagued by feelings of—it's hard to explain, but I couldn't see how my parents could really have loved me, yet put me through the hell they did. The hell of boarding school when you're only five, the hell of being the one in the middle, of my mother, who was a prize bitch,' he said coldly, 'trying to alienate me from my father, whom I loved. Of him letting her do it, perhaps not caring enough to try and stop her. Then—well, you grow up finally, thank God, and think you've put it all behind you and you discover you weren't the only kid in the world to suffer the trauma of divorce and separation. I thought I'd done that until I laid eyes on you. Then it all came back. I thought, he's prepared to be seen by some people as an old fool for this—*girl*, thirty years his junior, he's not going to let anything stand in his way with *her*. And he didn't either, did he, India? Nothing came between the two of you . . . Can you understand that I resented that?'

She stared at him with her lips parted, her eyes still wet and huge.

'Then he went one step further,' Giles Ballantyne said. 'He put you on the board of Ballantyne's, as if you were his own flesh and blood—even I, who was, had had to earn that.'

'Oh, God,' she said shakily then, 'I didn't really want it. I didn't ever want anything from him other than to be with him . . .' She stopped and bit her lip, then she forced herself to go on. 'It was a different way that he loved me . . .'

'Naturally,' Giles said drily, 'I'm not disputing that. Are you trying to say that because it was a sexual thing it had to be a stronger bond?'

'I . . . I'm trying to say that it had nothing whatsoever to do with—I mean, it didn't lessen his love for you. They were two things that could have gone along side by side if only you'd let them. They *did*, I knew that—why do you think I never told him how you treated me? Because he loved you and I knew it would only hurt him. Why do you think I've gone along with this . . .?' She stopped and closed her eyes.

'This what? Supporting me on the board bit?' he queried acutely.

She nodded after a moment.

'Yes, well,' he said at last, 'all this has belatedly begun to dawn on me. Also, the fact that you've very genuinely mourned him.'

India opened her eyes. 'Since when? Since this morning?'

'I . . .' he hesitated, and then smiled briefly. 'I can be very stubborn and pig-headed at times. However, a few weeks ago I bought one of your paintings—oh, I didn't even know it was yours, I didn't take much notice of the signature on it. All I knew was that it appealed to me very much, so much that I didn't mind forking out a fairly large sum for it. Then I had a dinner-party, and one of the guests commented on it and said he had an India Lawson too.'

India moved restlessly.

'Which led me to wonder,' he went on. 'I couldn't remember your maiden name, but I was quite sure there weren't too many Indias on the Gold Coast. So I went back to the gallery. With a bit of ... persuasion, they finally admitted that India Lawson and India Ballantyne were one and the same person.'

'I don't—I don't see what that's got to do with anything,' India said huskily.

'What I'm trying to say is that it dawned on me that you weren't entirely dependent on my father's ...'

'Charity?' she supplied.

'You said it—but what I meant was that if you kept on painting like that, or possibly had been for some time, you'd make a lot of money out of it. So that my threats to you would be a little meaningless.'

They eyed each other, and India licked her lips. 'That's not quite true,' she admitted honestly. 'I've only fairly recently begun to make money from my paintings. Also, well, I can't help knowing that what Rod left me, he really wanted me to have. And that he left you far, far, more. I can't see that it's right for you to want to take what I've got away from me. On the other hand I would have hated, still do, to go to court and fight you for it,' she said starkly.

He said nothing for a time. Then, 'The painting I bought was a self-portrait, I now realise.' And he glanced at the Abbot's chair. India took a breath. 'You can't recognise the girl sitting on the floor in it,' he continued, 'She's too shadowy. But the empty chair she's staring at so ... with an air of grief and disbelief somehow painted into those shadowy outlines ... the empty chair is quite recognisable as that chair.'

One week later India was sitting beside Giles as they drove up the Pacific Highway towards Brisbane.

It was latish on a bright, warm Sunday morning, the traffic was moderate, the boot of the car contained two sets of luggage, and India was still wondering with amazement, as she had been all week, why and quite how she'd been persuaded to do this.

For Rod's sake? For the sake of Rod's memory, rather ...

Yes, it had to be that, she mused, but she wasn't quite convinced. So she argued it out with herself—it appeared to be a genuine olive branch that Giles had offered. How, as someone who had loved his father and in the light of some of the things Giles had told her, could she have refused it?

'I could have said,' she murmured to herself, 'something like—all right, apologies and explanations accepted. That doesn't mean that because we're no longer sworn enemies, that we will now automatically *like* each other. And to spend a week on a tropical island in each other's company—it might even be a way of totally alienating us for ever!'

But she hadn't said that. I never *do* think of the right thing to say until it's too late, she thought.

But to make matters worse, she still had the niggling suspicion at the back of her mind that whatever she'd said, she'd have found herself out-manoeuvred and still be driving towards Brisbane airport this Sunday morning.

She sighed unconsciously as she stared out of the window.

'Penny for your thoughts, India?' Giles offered.

'Oh, nothing.' She turned her head and smiled uncertainly at him. How do you suddenly become on friendly terms with a man you've hated for five long years ... 'It's really warm, isn't it?'

'Mmm, and it will be warmer up there. I hope you've brought all your summery things?'

'Yes, I packed mostly shorts and things like that.'

'Did you put anything in for the evenings? There are four restaurants operating on Hamilton now—some are bound to be dressy.'

'Well—yes, a few.'

A spark of amusement lit his eyes as he glanced at her briefly. But he said gravely, 'I for one don't expect this to be all work and no play.' He flexed his shoulders. 'I'm overdue for a break, and this should be a good way to combine it with some work.'

India had been watching him through partly lowered lashes and something clicked in her mind, like a camera shutter working at high speed because of an excess of light. Only the light must have been so bright, in a manner of speaking, that she'd missed the view.

And all she was left with was a curiously nameless feeling of ... concern? Why, I wonder? she asked herself and twitched her hazel gaze straight ahead away from Giles Ballantyne who, for the first time in their association, wasn't wearing a conservative suit.

He had on a pair of buttery cream jeans, a light khaki-and-cream striped shirt with the broad stripes running across it and a khaki collar, and a pair of khaki canvas slip-on shoes.

Not that she'd have expected him to be dressed in a suit, she thought. One doesn't go to the tropics done up to the nines. And she herself was wearing a pair of blue jeans, superbly cut in the new baggier fashion about the hips, and teamed with a polyester silk shirt in a primrose yellow which was definitely going to be one of her favourite colours this season. She also had on a pair of flat navy shoes with a narrow yellow trim, and they'd been an inspired find because the yellow matched her shirt. She wore a large pair of navy-framed sunglasses and as usual, she had on a couple of fine gold necklaces, the chain she wore on her watch wrist and two rings, mainly because she'd forgotten to deposit them with the bank while she was away. Her emerald-and-diamond engagement ring, and on the little finger of her right hand a black opal that flashed with magnificent green and red fire when it caught the light. It wasn't a large stone, mounted on a narrow band of two gold strands that twisted around each other, but it was a very rare stone.

Her nails were beautifully manicured and painted a deep cherry-red, as were her lips. Because of her over-exposure to the sun the day of the board meeting her tan was slightly darker than normal, but it looked good because of the smoothness of her skin which only needed to be moisturised. And she'd had her hair shaped before coming away and—perhaps also something to do with the sun—there were chestnut lights in the cloud of dark curls.

But as they got closer to Brisbane she found herself, after that curious, camera-like sensation of her mind, wondering if the casual clothes Giles Ballantyne was wearing had altered his aura suddenly. Only they should make it less frightening, she thought. Shouldn't they? Not more . . .

And she sighed again though inwardly this time and was glad she had an excuse to wear her sunglasses—she was quite sure her hazel eyes would be looking anxious and puzzled.

They didn't talk much after that, other than to comment on the traffic that was streaming down the double highway in the opposite direction towards the coast, and on how the outskirts of Brisbane seemed to be creeping ever further south.

But as they were driving along Kingsford-Smith Drive, alongside the Brisbane River and the container wharves, he said suddenly, 'Did you bring your painting gear?'

'Not really, just a sketch pad and a box of water colours. But I brought my camera to jog my memory.'

'Good.' He sounded pleased and she looked at him enquiringly. He shrugged. 'I might be able to acquire an India Lawson hot off the press.'

'I doubt that. I'm not a fast painter,' she replied with a grin.

'Here we are,' he said a couple of minutes later as he nosed the car into a space outside the domestic departure terminal of Eagle Farm airport. 'Would you mind very much if I left you here with the luggage for a short time while I put the car into the security parking area? There's a courtesy bus back but it means . . .'

'No, I don't mind,' she said swiftly. 'I always used to do it for . . .' She broke off and bit her lip. *Do it for Rod*, she'd been going to say. 'Oh, there's a free trolley!' she added. 'I'll nip out and grab it.'

But while she waited beside the loaded trolley for Giles to return, instead of finding herself feeling sad and nostalgic, she was instead surprised to feel a little excited. Airports had always excited her, she remembered, although there were some aspects of flying that did not. But she was a fairly seasoned traveller now, seasoned enough to be able to keep her certain fears well to the back of her mind, but not that blasé to be unaffected by airports and the hustle and bustle, the roar of jets and that magic feeling of going off to somewhere new.

Giles appeared at her side and took control of the trolley. 'We'll check in and get rid of this stuff,' he said. 'Then I'll buy you a drink—it is Sunday lunchtime, after all.'

The airline clerk was very friendly. 'Mr . . . and Mrs Ballantyne,' he said with a beaming smile, as he scanned their tickets. 'How are you? Oh, you lucky couple, off to Hamilton Island! It's a great spot. Would you like to be in a smoking section or non on the aircraft?'

'Non,' Giles and India said simultaneously. 'But we're not . . .' India added looking fleetingly discomfited, 'I mean, well, it doesn't matter,' she murmured, and turned away with a faint flush in her cheeks, for a spark of speculation had leapt into the clerk's eyes. Now he thinks I'm not Mrs Ballantyne at all, she told herself, that I'm going away for an illicit holiday ... why did I open my mouth? Does it really matter whether he thinks Giles and I are married?

'I explained,' Giles told her a few minutes later, coming up to her where she stood a few steps away. His eyes were laughing. 'But I'm afraid to say he found that harder to believe if anything, although he didn't say so.'

India grimaced. 'I hope it doesn't keep happening. It hadn't dawned on me ... that it might be a natural assumption for people to make.'

'You could always revert to your maiden name,' he said abruptly, his eyes no longer laughing, 'if you're so worried about what people will think. I'm afraid I don't have one to fall back on. Ballantyne is the only one I've had.'

And I'm not going to change it for you, India, she imagined him adding in his mind, because for a moment she glimpsed all the old hostility and aggression that Giles Ballantyne was so capable of feeling towards her. She shivered slightly.

He stared at her with his mouth set, then it was as if he made himself relax. 'Let's get that drink I mentioned before it's too late,' he said lightly.

But the sense of constraint, that India had hoped her feeling of excitement might have dissipated, was back.

The Ansett jet gathered momentum and surged down the runway.

India, as always on take-off and although she had the window seat, stared down at her hands clasped in her lap. Taking off was never a happy time for her and somehow, to look out and see the ground receding and then to be banking over it, not very high up and at odd angles with your eardrums starting to feel thick, made it worse for her. So she always concentrated on her hands or the back of the seat in front of her at least, until the No Smoking and Fasten Seat Belts signs blinked off.

Rod had always laughed at her and held her hand.

Giles Ballantyne's strong, square-tipped hand hovered over her clenched fists briefly then descended to cover them. 'I'm sorry,' he said, 'I . . . well, I'm sorry. I took offence where there was no offence intended. I do that, unfortunately.'

India looked at him and heard herself saying, 'Oh—it's not really that.' She glanced at his strong hand covering hers. 'The truth is I'm very nervous about taking off in planes.'

Their eyes met, dark grey and hazel, and he lifted his eyebrows. 'I know it's silly,' she added awkwardly.

'I know, I keep telling myself that,' he said. 'But the thing is, most crashes . . .' He stopped.

'Happen while taking off or landing?' she supplied after a moment.

'Yes, but I was trying not to say that.'

'Do you mean—you suffer from it too?'

'Regrettably,' he confessed wryly.

'I thought I was the only person in the world who . . .'

'No.'

'Well, I mean I didn't really believe that, but everyone else seems so cool. You can't pick them, can you? I couldn't have picked you for example.'

'You weren't looking at me,' he said with an

amused lift of his eyebrows. 'That's why I thought you were angry with me.'

'I—no, I'm not, really,' she said a little hesitantly, and her hands stirred beneath his.

But he didn't take it away. 'Not really?' he queried.

'Giles,' she bit her bottom lip with her very white, even teeth, a habit which Rod had found particularly endearing, 'it's just a little hard to accept this . . . state of affairs, I guess. I mean, it might take a bit of getting used to.' She looked at him helplessly.

'Of course,' he agreed gravely. 'Why, only a week ago you wanted to hit me with my own paperweight—a deadly weapon, I'm sure, if used in the right way.'

'How did you know?' she asked involuntarily.

He shrugged and said with a wicked gleam in his eyes, 'You looked at it with such longing.'

India couldn't help herself, she had to smile and look rueful at the same time. 'I didn't realise I was *that* transparent,' she murmured.

'Actually, I thought you contained yourself admirably, but let's not go backwards.' His grip on her hands tightened briefly. 'All right?'

'A-all right,' she agreed and to her certain confusion, found herself smiling at him again, unable to help herself but at the same time with an oddly sinking feeling. As if there were an element of danger in the fact that Giles Ballantyne could be so nice. But why? she wondered.

The stewardess interrupted her thoughts. They both looked up, still with their hands together, and Giles must have seen, as India did, her immediate assumption that she had a pair of lovers in seats

14A and B, because he flashed India a look that said clearly and laughingly, here we go again!

And India found herself laughing back at him.

The flight to Hamilton Island took almost an hour and a half.

After lunch Giles read a Sunday paper and India sat back and watched the passing landscape below, feeling relaxed, a little sleepy from the glass of wine she'd had and experiencing a mild sense of anticipation. I haven't had a holiday for a long time either, she thought. And you couldn't find a more beautiful part of the world to have one in, could you?

The plane was descending as it crossed the coastline in the area of Mackay and she glimpsed the Hay Point terminal that stretched far out to sea to load the giant tankers with coal from the rich inland Queensland fields.

Then it was like floating down into a wonderland of dark green islands studding a sea of almost breathtaking beauty—stretched like aquamarine silk, with darker patches that indicated the presence of coral reefs. The lower they got, the more enchanted she was as she could pick out white beaches fringing the islands, secluded bays, yachts at anchor, one rather forbidding-looking island with a high sheer rocky point on it tinged pink in the sunlight . . .

'That's Pentecost Island,' Giles said over her shoulder. 'Captain Cook, as you probably know, discovered the passage through these islands in early June, hence the names. We must be very close now.'

The captain's disembodied voice confirmed this.

They would be landing on Hamilton Island in a few minutes.

India came out of her reverie slightly as she saw the airstrip float by, then felt the plane bank steeply, for the airstrip on Hamilton Island was bounded on both ends by the sea. 'It doesn't look very long,' she said a shade nervously.

'It's long enough,' Giles replied, and took her hand. 'It certainly reduces the trip, this airstrip. Before this was opened you had to fly to Prosperpine then get to Shute Harbour to take a boat, or do the last leg by helicopter. There, we're down,' he said as the jets roared into reverse. 'Came down like a feather, didn't we? And he's going to stop in plenty of time.'

India grinned a little weakly. 'I am a fool.'

'Just remind yourself you're not the only one.'

She looked at him doubtfully.

'I don't mind landing—once I know the wheels have come down and you can usually feel that, I feel quite safe. Well, welcome to Hamilton, India. Shall we disembark?'

The air outside the aircraft was bright and hot. The small terminal building wasn't yet completed, and a man with a megaphone was doing the honours—into this bus guests of Hamilton Island, that one people transferring to Hayman, et cetera.

Their bus driver was a bright young man who collected up his flock and said cheerfully, as he put the bus into gear to cope with steep gradient away from the airfield, 'Right, folks, what I'll do is drive you all to Reception first, where you can check in. Then if you'd all like to meet back at the bus, I'll take you round to your respective accommodation.

What you see on your left-hand side now is
Hamilton Harbour, and that green building there
is the Mariners' Inn—a fine pub that serves meals
too! There are two stores nearby for condominium
guests, and any odds and ends you might need.
We're now,' he paused as he negotiated a couple
of bends, 'commencing a descent,' he said
playfully, 'to the other side of the island. On your
right,' India looked out at two cream-painted,
several-storied buildings, 'are the condominiums
set up on the hill a little, and these are the *bures*-
style accommodation starting now. The Outrigger
hotel is up there on your left. This,' he drove the
bus under a portico, 'is Reception!'

'It's very big,' India said a little bewilderedly to
Giles.

'And going to get bigger,' he answered wryly.
'There's still a lot of construction under way and a
lot that hasn't been started. Do you want to stay
here while I check in?'

'I—no. I'd like to see Reception. It looks very
impressive!'

It was impressive, she discovered as she stared
around the main reception area. The ceiling soared
upwards like the inside of a hollow pyramid but
with a flat top, and was lined with panelling and
beams of a reddish wood. Below the ceiling was a
frieze of copper and wood decorative plaques. The
central floor area was on a lower level and
dominated by a stand of large lush plants that
grew high, and were surrounded by a low marble
wall inset with luxurious settees. And there was an
outer circle of marble niches, again set with settees
and tables and lamps. A step down beyond this
gave wide open access to the huge pool with a

palm-studded island in it and a suspension bridge across it. Beyond the pool, which looked sparkling clear and inviting, you could walk down to the beach.

India glanced back and seeing that there was still a crowd around Reception, she walked a little way out into the sunlight and turned to look back at the building.

It was L-shaped, she discovered, with three of those high, truncated pyramid style roofs sheathed in red cedar shingles that were weathering to a silvery grey. The one over the reception area formed the base corner of the L, and the other two were at either end of the building. The short arm of the building appeared to be taken up with restaurants and lounges, and there was a deep, fairly narrow pool in front of them. The longer arm wasn't quite finished at the end, but from the reception area there was a broad, paved walkway with, so far, three superbly elegant shopfronts facing on to it. A ladies' boutique, a gentleman's called Lord Nelson's and a jewellery shop with some of the most exquisite coral jewellery she'd ever seen in its windows. It was called—appropriately for two reasons—Lady Hamilton's.

'I'm impressed!' she murmured to herself as she strolled back into Reception. 'It could be a hard act to follow.'

'What's that?' Giles queried, looming up in front of her.

'Oh,' she smiled wryly, 'I was just thinking that whoever designed this knew what they were about! A distinct Polynesian influence, I would say, of course on a grander scale but still conveying a—how can I put it? A sense of the South Pacific? Of open-sided meeting houses and balmy nights and beachcombers . . .' She stopped, because Giles was looking at her rather intently. 'What's wrong?' she asked warily.

'Nothing. Something very right. You've summed this place up perfectly. That's why I brought you here, Mrs Ballantyne.'

'You're not intending to copy it? Is that what you mean?'

'Not at all. I meant that it was because of your perception of styles and places, that I brought you here.'

'Oh well,' India replied with a grin, 'do you think in that case you could rustle me up a cup of tea? I really feel like one to—lubricate my perceptions. Which you vastly over-estimate, Giles,' she added.

'Done!' he replied. 'The bus is waiting to take us to our rooms. We can have a cup of tea there.'

Their rooms were next door to each other in the main hotel buildings of the Outrigger Resort and from her verandah, India was able to get a much better impression of the whole of this side of the island. And it was a rather magical setting she gazed out over. The resort was curved about a lagoon with a sandy beach and because it was high tide, the water was dotted with wind-surfers, the colourful sails of small catamarans, swimmers and ski-board surfers. There was a huge rock pool at the opposite end of the beach and beyond it, a steep, green-clad hill arced about the lagoon to a high, rocky point—Passage Peak it was called, she discovered from the literature she'd found in the room. And the beach was called Catseye Beach taking its name from the curious shells that looked like cat's eyes, found there.

The ridge that ended in Passage Peak curved back across the island to descend to the harbour although you couldn't see that side of the island, and formed the backdrop for the condominium buildings —units, in other words, that could be bought.

Another ridge formed the second arm about the lagoon and ended in a smooth dome with one lone tree on it—One Tree Hill—and the hotel buildings backed on to this ridge.

But perhaps the most interesting form of accommodation on Hamilton Island, India decided, were the *bures*, individual little buildings with high-pointed green roofs and wide front verandahs set in curving lines behind the main reception building, amid trees and sloping lawns. Each one was self-contained, the literature said, and they were certainly very attractive and added to the Polynesian style of things.

But the focal point, especially when viewed from higher up as she was doing now, was the unique main building with its pyramid domes, palm trees and of course the huge swimming-pool it surrounded—the largest in the Pacific, she read, and realised that the island in it, with its thatched shelters, was also a swim-up bar, and contained a sauna.

'Now that's what I call luxury,' she murmured, and jumped as someone knocked on the door.

It was Giles, with two cups balanced awkwardly in one hand. 'Tea, ma'am?' he said. 'Or have you made your own?'

'Not yet,' she confessed. 'I haven't even started to unpack. I've been gazing out at the view.'

'It's some view,' he commented, and came in. 'Like your room?'

'Yes—ah, thanks.' She accepted the cup from him. 'Yes, they're very nice.' She looked around. The room was in fact a bed-sitting-room with cool, tiled floors, a huge double bed covered in a tailored green quilt, a settee and two chairs, a glass-topped coffee table, several lamps and a built-in unit which contained a small fridge, stocked to almost overflowing with soft drinks and mineral water, and the facilities to make tea and coffee. There was also a wide variety of alcoholic drinks available.

On one wall there was a fabric printed map of Hamilton Island and the Whitsundays, and on another a lovely print of a hibiscus flower.

The bathroom, she had discovered, had every mod. con., including a hair-dryer and in a cupboard she'd discovered an iron and ironing board.

'I thought we might go for a swim,' Giles said. 'What did you have in mind?'

'The same,' she replied draining her cup. 'How could you resist it?'

CHAPTER FOUR

'STILL feeling all right?' Giles asked.

They were having lunch on the open verandah of the Beach Bar and Grill above the beach. The tide was coming in and India had been amazed at how far it went out—you could walk out for several hundred yards to where the sandy bottom gave way to ridges of coral, and so the three pontoons closer in rested on the sand.

'I'm fine, really I am,' she said.

'You're not making much headway with your lunch,' he observed.

'That's only because it's enormous,' she answered laughingly, and eyed the T-bone steak which was as big as her plate and only half-eaten so far, and the chips and wooden bowl heaped with a variety of mouth-watering salads that Giles had procured for her. 'I'm sorry about last night,' she said, 'but it was only because I was really tired—I don't quite know why but not that I was sick or anything.'

The fact was, she mused, it *was* a bit of a mystery to her that she should have been so tired. Tired enough after they'd come back from their swim, to barely unpack before lying down on the wide bed to fall deeply asleep although it had only been six o'clock. It's not that she wasn't used to the sea air or the water, she was. It must have been the trip.

Unfortunately they'd arranged to have dinner at the Outrigger Restaurant but Giles, knocking repeatedly on her door, had not woken her.

'Can't understand how I slept through it,' she said ruefully, and bit into a tiny, mayonnaise-covered potato from the salad bowl, that had been cooked in its jacket. 'I haven't been sleeping well since . . . well, for a long time now. I generally get up and paint for a couple of hours every night.'

'It's just as well I didn't know that. I'd have been tempted to get the management to check up on you. But it did occur to me you were tired. On the other hand, I was rather relieved when you answered your door this morning. Another glass of wine?'

He held the carafe of ruby-red liquid poised.

'Oh well, why not! But I shall soon have to be doing a lot of activity to compensate for all this food and wine at lunchtime. You could easily get fat living like this!'

His dark grey gaze skimmed her figure that was not particularly revealed because she had a matching blouse on over her white swimsuit, white too and patterned with sprays of the same brilliant coral, sapphire and emerald green flowers and leaves. Against her tan and dark hair the dazzling white of the Lycra looked superb, and she'd been the recipient of many an admiring glance around the pool earlier.

And for a moment she thought Giles was going to make an admiring comment and held her breath, she wasn't sure why. But all he said eventually was, 'I might take you up on that. How about a game of tennis after we've given our lunch a chance to settle? The tide will be in enough to swim afterwards—a good way to cool down. Did you bring any sandshoes? Not that it matters, you can hire them.'

India cast him a slightly wary glance and was suddenly consumed by a sense of unreality. Is this really—us? Giles and India Ballantyne sharing lunch and more? A sense of relaxed companionship and a total lack of formality? He too was wearing swimming togs, dark blue fitting board shorts, and he'd pulled on a pale pink T-shirt.

'What's wrong?' he said.

'Wrong—nothing,' she said a little disjointedly then managed to slip into another gear. She wrinkled her nose. 'I did bring some sandshoes, but for walking on the coral. I . . . I'm not a very good tennis player. So I don't accept challenges where I suspect I might be beaten rotten.' She looked at him enquiringly.

His lips twitched but he said gravely, 'I'm only average myself.'

India sighed and murmured, 'Everyone says that. Then you get on the court with them and discover they're Rod Lavers or Chris Evert-Lloyds. But,' she sat up, 'never mind, the exercise will do me good! You're on.'

'You see, I was right,' India declared, later that afternoon as she sat sprawled and trying to get her breath beside the tennis court, 'Average!' she said scornfully. 'You're as bad as your father, he used to beat me . . .' She stopped and bit her lip.

'India,' Giles squatted down beside her, all the laughter which their rather one-sided set had brought to his eyes, wiped away suddenly, 'we can't not talk about him.'

'I . . . wasn't sure that you'd like to hear me talking about him,' she said very quietly, turning her racquet over in her hands. She lifted her hazel eyes suddenly. 'Or that I want to talk ... to you about him.'

Their gaze searched each other's eyes and there was something in his that puzzled her, something a little harsh. *I wonder if he still suspects that I was on the make ...?*

'The point is,' Giles said finally, and equally quietly, 'that's going backwards. The other thing is, he featured so prominently in both our lives. If we both stop short when he comes to mind, it'll be like a barrier between us for ever.'

'He was the reason there ever was one.'

'I know. But I thought we'd agreed to ...'

She stood up suddenly. 'I can't—I just can't wipe it all out as if it never happened,' she said, her voice clogged with distress.

'I'm not asking you to do that,' he said, standing up and turning her to face him.

'Yes you are,' she whispered. 'You want me to talk about him ...'

'I don't, precisely,' he interrupted, and there was a fleeting look of irony in his eyes, but so swiftly did it come and go, she thought she must have imagined it. 'What I do want,' he went on very evenly, 'is for you not to look guilty every time his name comes up.'

'It's not *guilt*,' she said. 'It could never be that—it's the fact that you tried to debase something that was the nicest thing that ever happened to me. I loved him and he loved me, but you tried to turn it into something else. An old man with a young girl, a fortune huntress ... it wasn't like that.'

'I tried to tell you that I came to understand that, India.'

'I know ...'

'You can't believe me, then.'

She put a hand to her mouth. 'I want to,' she said indistinctly. 'I really want to, for his sake . . .'

'And your own?' he queried.

She stared at him blindly. 'Perhaps it will just take time,' she said huskily. 'It's not . . .' She sighed, and tried again. 'You've been very nice to be with, and that's strange I suppose—I mean, strange to me, or *confusing* perhaps.' She stopped, then added, 'That seems to put it in a nutshell, I feel confused, but then I never was particularly bright.'

He smiled slightly. 'Brighter than you know,' he said barely audibly. 'Do you want to go home?'

'I . . . no,' she said uncertainly.

'Then shall we just muddle through as best we can?'

She stared at him. 'Oughtn't we . . . I mean, when are we going to see the island? And didn't you say you had an architect and a surveyor coming?'

He grimaced. 'If we got to work it would help, is that what you're trying to say?'

'Well, we did come here to do that.'

'Wednesday—they're arriving on Wednesday. That means there's only the rest of today and tomorrow to be got through.'

'Giles,' she put out a hand, feeling suddenly churlish, 'I'm sorry, I'm being a twit, I guess. The trouble is, the real trouble I think, is that I still *miss* Rod so much. Which is not your fault or your problem. And perhaps because it's been such a lonely time, I've got into the habit of feeling depressed and sorry for myself.' She half-smiled.

His eyes narrowed. 'Haven't you got any friends?'

'Well, no,' she confessed, 'I never did make friends easily. Rod ... was my friend as well as everything else. Oh, I've got people I talk to, the old lady who lives next door, the girl in the paper shop—people like that ...'

She stopped, surprised into silence by the curiously bleak look she saw in his eyes. 'What is it?' she asked.

He closed his eyes briefly. 'Nothing. I think I've got the picture ... Well, if you're sure you want to stay, shall we go for the swim we promised ourselves?' He held out a hand.

'... Yes,' she said, and put her fingers into his.

Several hours later, India regarded herself in the wide bathroom mirror and thought she looked unusually well.

She'd dressed for dinner in a green silky frock with narrow shoulder straps, a blouson bodice and a straight skirt. She wore an unusual gold belt with it, wide at the front and tapering to the back, and gold, high-heeled sandals.

Not that I usually look sick, she reflected, so where does the difference lie? Is it a look of anticipation? A complete change of mood? Could be, despite my confusion about the company. After all, the only occasions I've dressed up for for ages have been board meetings. And I've eaten a river of meals on my own ... yes, must be that!

She reached for her purse as a knock sounded on the door, and opened the door at the same time retrieving her power key and saying lightly, 'She's awake!'

'Bingo,' Giles replied with a grin.

* * *

'Giles! Why, Giles Ballantyne, is that you?'

Giles and India were just in the process of being seated in the Outrigger Restaurant, with its distinctive Polynesian high-raked roof, when this male voice rang out.

Giles turned and was all but engulfed by a very large young man with snapping dark eyes and a thatch of wild fair hair. 'Brad!' he said, laughing. 'What the hell are you doing here?'

'Now is that any way to greet your best buddy?' Brad replied, still shaking Giles's hand vigorously.

The next few minutes were confused. Brad had a lady companion, a petite girl with the exquisite face of a doll but twinkling, humorous-looking eyes. India gathered that Brad and Giles had been to school together—the hovering waiter apparently gathered that it was a fairly momentous reunion too, because he finally suggested that they join forces and share a table—he had a larger one available, he murmured.

'That's a great idea!' Brad said enthusiastically. He exuded enormous enthusiasm, also the certain over-powering quality of a large, shaggy dog, so the change-over was accomplished with some confusion but finally they were sitting around a table for four, and India for one was feeling a little breathless.

Not so Brad. He subsided into his chair then immediately sat forward. 'This is Petula,' he said. 'Petula, meet Giles Ballantyne, the fastest winger the Under Seventeens ever saw ... Petula is my lady!'

Petula smiled unembarrassedly and murmured hello.

'Your turn, Giles!' Brad commanded, but before

Giles had a chance to speak, he turned to India and said sincerely, 'You're about the loveliest thing I've ever laid eyes on, and I'm sure Petula here will agree with me. I must say Giles always had great taste in girls but you beat the lot of 'em!'

India's smile wavered but it was to get worse. Brad's admiring gaze then lit upon her wedding ring. 'Oh, by Jove!' he exclaimed loudly, 'when did this happen? This calls for champagne—waiter! Sorry, ma'am,' he added contritely to India, 'shouldn't have mentioned all the other girls, not done, is it? But you don't have a thing to worry about . . .'

'Brad,' Giles said, 'India and I are not married.'

'Not? Oops, here I go again. I have a terrible habit of putting my foot into things. By the way I'm Brad Mortimer . . . India,' he said. 'What a lovely name! What goes with it?'

'Ballantyne,' Giles said resignedly, and added to his friend's comical look of confusion, 'India was married to my father. She's in fact—yes, my stepmother. We're here on business.'

A curious thing happened then. Brad Mortimer blinked, shook his head and started to laugh, saying at the same time, 'I'm terribly sorry, but you two must admit you present a trap for the unwary! My deepest apologies, India. Will you forgive me?'

The old resentment had begun to course through India's veins—the bottom line, as she sometimes thought of it, and it wasn't that she'd been mistaken for Giles's wife, although that was bad enough. No, it always came back to the fact that she'd been married to a man so much older than herself. That's what really threw people and

made them regard her with speculation, if not
outright suspicion. It was the thing she hated most
of all, the thing she'd been naïve enough not to
expect, only she'd seen it so often over the past
five years that she had no difficulty in recognising
it.

Yet there seemed to be something so genuine
about this friend of Giles, she found herself
thinking suddenly, of course it would be an easy
mistake to make, why read more into it? It's
probably funny too—in fact I'd rather he laughed
than looked embarrassed . . .

'That's all right,' she said. 'But I'm thinking of
getting myself a little name badge with the family
tree printed on it!'

That did the trick, she discovered. Giles relaxed
imperceptibly, and they all laughed together. And
the ice was well and truly broken—Brad and
Petula had only arrived that afternoon but were
staying a week, and were delighted at the prospect
of Giles's and India's company. At least so Brad
said jovially and Petula agreed.

'We do have some work to do,' Giles warned
with a grin.

'Oh, forget about work!' Brad dismissed it with
a wave of his hand. 'Hey, they tell me there's a
disco operating tonight over at the Mariners' Inn.
What say we pay it a visit after we've eaten?'

Giles gave India an interrogative look.

'It's fine with me,' she said after hesitating
fractionally.

'It's a good way of working off a meal,' he said
with a glint of amusement.

'Mariners', as it appeared to be affectionately

known, was sparking by the time they arrived. It was the favourite nightspot of staff members and frequented too by guests of the resort and people off the yachts moored in the harbour.

They found a table on the broad verandah and Brad insisted on ordering them all Piña Coladas. You could see inside to the small dance floor, the crowded bar, the tables, but have the advantage of the cooler night air.

That was until Brad stood up and held his hand out to India. 'Got to dance,' he said imperatively. 'This beat is driving me wild!'

India hesitated again and looked at Petula. 'Oh, please,' Petula laughed, 'dance with him! He's insatiable!'

'I . . .' Why am I stalling? India wondered. I love this beat too, but Rod used to hate the noise of discos so . . .

But she was given no further chance to stall. Brad Mortimer leaned down, put his hands around her waist, swung her out of her chair as if she were a feather and breathed into her ear in a throaty whisper, 'You got rhythm, lady. I can tell!'

'I'm sure you can't,' she protested, but was inexorably manoeuvred inside. And yet there was something about Brad that made it impossible to take offence—a sort of friendly, puppy-like quality. I wonder if Petula constantly thinks of him in doggy terms? India thought briefly, and with a smile curving her lips.

Then they were on the dance floor and she begun to feel nervous again. But her partner was not to be gainsaid, and after a few fumbles, India found herself doing the incredible—letting her hair down metaphorically, doing her own thing, which actually appeared to coincide with what Brad was doing, and surrendering herself to the music unselfconsciously and with marvellous enjoyment.

She saw Giles and Petula dancing by and waved. Giles was looking at her quizzically, she noted vaguely.

But finally, she ran out of steam and begged her partner to take her back to the table. 'Petula was right about you!' she accused, gasping slightly. 'Besides, we're not being very polite, are we?'

Brad grinned down at her. 'Okay. And I was right about you. You do have rhythm.'

'If you only knew ...' She didn't finish her sentence but he didn't seem to notice, just took her hand and led her back to the table and then went in search of fresh drinks.

Giles and Petula were there and India noticed again that Giles was looking at her quizzically.

But Petula said warmly, 'You were great! I can see I'll have to brush up, or I'll lose my partner altogether!'

'Oh, I'm so sorry!' India looked at her worriedly. 'I don't know what got into me. I haven't danced like that—well, never, really.'

'Never?' Giles queried.

'No. It's very strange ...'

'No it's not. It's Brad,' Petula put in. 'He has that effect on people. Oh God, I think it's my turn now!'

It was. Brad put India's drink down on the table, took a long pull of his and crooked his finger at Petula.

'It must be that,' India said, looking wry and a little relieved as the other two disappeared inside.

'I mean it must be Brad. But the funny thing is I never realised how I longed to ... to ...' She broke off, and her eyes widened painfully.

'Break out?' Giles suggested finally. 'I gather my father wasn't much of a fan of this kind of thing?'

'No.'

'It's no crime to enjoy it even if he didn't, India.'

'I suppose not ...'

'Then why are you looking so glum?' There was a slightly sharp note in his voice.

'I feel ... as if I've been disloyal to him,' she admitted eventually, and toyed with her glass.

He sat forward. 'That's ridiculous. Do you think he'd have expected you to spend the rest of your life in purdah?'

'Oh no, but ... well, he didn't even really like me dancing with anyone else.' Her eyelashes flew up, as if she'd just made this discovery. 'I mean,' she said uncertainly, 'it wasn't anything he ever said, but I ... sort of knew.'

Giles looked at her steadily. Then he said drily, 'Some husbands don't.'

'Would you—if you had a wife?' she asked.

A sudden flicker of amusement lit his eyes. 'I might wait until I acquire one before I make any sweeping statements on the matter. The thing is ...' He shrugged but didn't go on.

'What?'

He said with another shrug, 'I was going to point out that he's no longer with us—you, but I don't suppose you'll appreciate me saying that.'

'No ...'

'I didn't think you would.'

'I meant—no, he isn't, and I suppose it's silly to

be afraid of enjoying myself,' she said perplexedly. 'Is that what I'm doing?'

He lifted an eyebrow. 'You could hardly be enjoying yourself in a more innocent manner. For one thing you're *young* and, I suspect, livelier than you appear on the surface. There's nothing wrong with that.'

India pulled a face. 'You sound like the oracle. And I know I appear quite dumb sometimes—no, I'm not taking offence!' She grinned at the surprise on Giles's face. 'But it's suddenly dawned on me I've become a bit of a bore. Must be these Piña Coladas—I'm not sure if I like them, but I'm quite sure it's powerful stuff!'

'You've only had one and a half,' he pointed out sceptically.

She turned her head and gazed out over the harbour, at the yachts with their furled sails and the power craft, some with lights on that reflected on the dark water. 'Then it must be the moonlight,' she said a little dreamily. 'But whatever, I've just discovered I'm really not in the mood to be glum! Would *you* like to dance with me . . .?' She turned back as soon as the words had left her mouth. *Dear God, India, what's got into you? But it's true I don't feel like being sad . . .*

He said with his lips twitching, 'If you don't think you'll hate yourself, and me, in the morning, I'd like to very much.'

She had to laugh. 'I promise . . .'

'I could have danced all night!' Petula sang as the four of them trudged up the hill from Mariners. 'Whose idea was it to walk back, by the way?' she added.

'Yours!' they all answered.

'I was afraid of that—I had a good reason for it but I can't think of it now. I *think* I'm a bit tipsy,' she said confidingly.

'I *know* it!' Brad replied. 'And that's why you wanted to walk, my precious idiot.'

'Don't be cross with me,' she said, snuggling up to Brad like a kitten. 'All those Piña Coladas were *your* idea . . . oh, thank God for that! I do believe we've hit the top and the rest is all downhill!'

'Stop a minute and catch your breath,' Brad advised.

They all stopped and India said dreamily, 'What a beautiful night, and what a super mango tree!'

Giles looked at her with a glimmer of a smile.

'Well it is, isn't it?' She pointed upwards at the giant tree that stood on the crest of the hill between the harbour and the beach side of the island. It also stood at a crossroad—where roads led to the staff quarters and in the opposite direction to the condominiums and the airport. 'I wonder if they call this Mango Tree Corner?'

'We can suggest it to them,' Giles said gravely and reached for her hand. 'Feeling tipsy too?'

India considered. 'No,' she said finally. 'Just relaxed, tired but nicely so—I've had a wonderful evening!'

'So have I,' he agreed after a moment. They'd started to walk again.

'You're a pretty hot dancer yourself,' India murmured.

'Ah, but unlike you, I've taken years to perfect it. You're a natural . . .'

'This is it, folks,' Brad interrupted. '*Bure* number ten—where are you two staying?'

'Up at the hotel. We'll say good night then . . .'

'Brad, I can't walk another step,' Petula interrupted. 'You've *danced* me to exhaustion . . .'

'Here you go, baby,' Brad said easily, and swung her up into his arms. She wound her arms round his neck and laid her head on his shoulder. 'I still love you,' she murmured sleepily.

Brad cocked an eye at Giles and India over his shoulder. 'See you folks in the morning!' he said with a grin.

'She's nice, isn't she?' India asked warmly as they moved off, still hand in hand. 'They both are.'

'Mmm . . . Not far to go now.'

They climbed the steps to the hotel building and then two more flights inside. It was very quiet and their footsteps echoed on the tiles. 'Got your key?' Giles asked.

India stopped and searched through her purse. 'Yes.'

He took it from her. 'By the way, I've booked us on a helicopter trip to the Reef tomorrow.'

She stiffened and looked up at him wide-eyed.

'And before you say anything,' he went on, 'it's perfectly safe, and it's a marvellous way of seeing the Reef and the other islands. I promise you won't regret it.'

'But . . .'

'But nothing.' He touched a finger to her mouth, 'you're a big, brave girl now, aren't you?'

'That's blackmail,' she said with a smile trembling on her lips. 'If I'm so brave, why didn't you tell me about it earlier?'

'I reasoned that the less time you had to think about it . . .'

'Then why tell me now? I've got all night!'

'Unfortunately the tide has conspired against me—we have to be ready at half-past six. But I've got the feeling you'll sleep like a top tonight.' They stopped opposite India's door and he opened it and inserted the power key into its socket so that the lights came on.

'Oh, well,' India said, 'I think you might be right. I'll let tomorrow take care of itself.' She yawned delicately, then grinned and on an impulse put her hand over his. 'Thanks,' she said, 'it was great!'

'Thank you ...' His fingers curled round hers and he lifted her hand to his mouth and kissed it.

'I ...' she said, but found that her voice was queerly unsteady and that, of all things, she was suddenly desperately conscious of Giles Ballantyne, of his hand around hers, the feel of his lips still on it although he'd lifted his head, of his body and the warmth and the grace and the strength of it—of the fact that she was conscious of a desire to be held in his arms and thoroughly kissed ...

She snatched her hand away, mumbled something incomprehensible but which ended on good night, and whisked herself inside, closing the door decisively.

CHAPTER FIVE

'No,' she whispered, leaning back against the door with her heart pounding like a train, 'I don't believe it. Oh, *stop*!'

She put her hands to her head to still the camera-like sensation she'd experienced once before. Only the picture was clear now, even if it was still incredible to her. Rather the series of pictures clicking away . . .

Giles Ballantyne on the trip up to the airport—that was when the first warning had sounded, because subconsciously she'd suddenly been aware of him not as an enemy, not someone to be feared and hated, but as a man, and she'd been unable to understand her vaguely fearful feeling. But she understood it only too well now. It had been a warning signal and she'd experienced it again on the plane because he could be so nice. . . .

This afternoon, she thought distractedly, after our game of tennis, what did I say? That I was *confused*. How right I was! she marvelled. But it's not only because Giles can be nice, it's because . . . because I've gone from hating him to being attracted to him in a matter of a few short days. How *could* I?

She pushed herself away from the door and walked unsteadily into the bathroom to stare at herself in the mirror. Her eyes were wide and horrified, her hair slightly dishevelled from dancing, her lips parted in disbelief.

'How could I?' She said the words aloud and closed her eyes. But instead of blotting anything out an insidious image floated behind her eyelids—of Giles picking her up as Brad had Petula, and carrying her into some dim, shadowy place and laying her on a bed, undressing her slowly, kissing her, touching . . .

Her eyes flew open and she didn't have to see the flood of colour that poured into her cheeks, she could feel it. All the same, she turned away from the mirror, her body feeling hot and cold with the shame of it. She hugged herself in a kind of agony and laid her forehead against the cool, tiled wall.

She stayed like that for an age then she straightened. 'I've got to think this out,' she whispered. 'I just can't believe . . . it.'

She undressed mechanically and took a brief shower, and slid into a sea-green silk nightgown. Then she made herself a cup of coffee and took it to bed, turning out all the lights save the bedside one, so that when she slipped into bed, she was sitting in a pool of golden light with the rest of the room dim.

She sat for a long time with her coffee-cup held in both hands, her head bent. Then she sighed and sipped her coffee and rested her head back.

It's not *Giles*, she thought. It's a combination of things, of loneliness, of this holiday atmosphere, of being surrounded by lovers—well, in their close company tonight anyway—of being a little tipsy, perhaps, although I feel stone cold sober now. And maybe it's because I've . . . known love. Does that make you more susceptible to it? Not that *this* is love, it can only be a sort of chemical reaction, surely?

But if anyone had told me I'd fall for virtually the first attractive man I came across, so soon after you left me, Rod, I'd never have believed them. And the irony of it being Giles—oh *God*! What will I *do*?

She licked her lips, and they were salty from the slow tears of anguish trickling down her cheeks.

It was six-fifteen when the telephone beside her bed rang. She was up and dressed in white shorts, a pumpkin coloured cotton shirt and white sand-shoes, and she'd tied her hair back with a white ribbon. Beside her on the bed was a straw hold-all neatly packed with a towel, a floppy linen hat, some sunscreen lotion, her camera . . .

She picked up the phone. '. . . Hello?'

'India? It's Giles. It's about a quarter past six.'

'I know. I'm ready.'

There was a slight pause. Then he said, 'Good. I was afraid you'd chicken out.'

'No.'

'I'll pick you up in a few minutes, then. I'm afraid you've got the drop on me this time. Say five minutes?'

'Fine . . .' She put the phone down and sat staring at her tanned knees. If you must know, Giles, she thought, dicing with death in a helicopter this morning quite matches my mood. I'm too numb even to feel nervous . . .

She stood up abruptly. Now look here, she said to herself sternly, I worked it all out last night, didn't I? It was *nothing*. Other than a brief spasm of the senses, probably induced by moonlight,

music and Piña Colada—which I will never
indulge in again. Right! Right . . .

'Are you all right?'

They were strolling across the dewy grass
towards the airline office. There was not a cloud in
the sky, and a promise of heat in the still, clear air.
Giles wore yellow shorts, a pale green T-shirt and,
like India, snowy white sandshoes. His gear was
packed into a small canvas duffle bag slung over
his shoulder. The early sunlight glinted on his
tawny hair and the golden hairs on his bare arms
and legs, and India's stomach had plummeted
when, after waiting five minutes, she'd come out of
her room to find him leaning against the wall
beside her door with his hand raised to knock and
his eyes still sleepy.

But she'd taken firm control of herself and greeted
him normally, she hoped. Now, she couldn't help
wondering how normal she'd sounded after all.

She said, 'I'm fine! Why shouldn't I be?' And
tried to infuse her expression with gaiety. *I mean,
all he can think about last night is that I got
embarrassed at having my hand kissed . . .*

He glanced at her briefly. 'You were up bright
and early.'

'I . . . it was the cockatoos,' she said with sudden
inspiration. 'A flock of them.' This was partially
true. She had heard a flock of cockatoos
squawking—in fact she'd seen them, white and
yellow, flying across the dawn-pink tinged bush
because she'd been awake already. 'I've been reading
up about this trip,' she went on. 'Apparently the
helicopter lands on a pontoon beside the Reef,' she
grimaced comically at him, 'and they take you off in

a glass-bottomed boat to see the coral.'

He grinned lazily. 'Sounds incredibly daring, doesn't it?'

'Sounds frightening to me!'

'Have you ever snorkelled?'

'Yes I have as a matter of fact—I'll enjoy that part at least.'

'Good.' He reached for her hand quite naturally and because she'd vowed to be perfectly natural herself, India didn't resist.

It was the same friendly courier who had collected them at the airport, though looking a little sleepy himself, who was waiting for them at the airline office with a bus.

'Great, you're all on time!' he said in some surprise. There were three other people assembled as well. 'We'll go and collect the snorkelling gear first and then get you over to the airport.'

The helicopter was small, with *Hamilton Island* painted on its sides in large letters. The pilot was looking a little worried as they arrived, India noted, but when he discovered that breakfast had arrived with them, his expression lightened. 'Thought I wasn't going to be able to *feed* you!' he said, and proceeded to demonstrate the life-jackets they had to wear, like belts with a pouch at the front. Then they were in the helicopter with the doors shut and the pilot was advising them to wear the earphones provided because of the noise, and because they'd be able to hear him talking.

It was small and cramped inside the passenger compartment although there were only four of them, the fifth person sitting beside the pilot. And the noise was very loud as the helicopter warmed up, even with the headphones which were uncomfortable. And the warming-up process seemed to take an age . . .

Oh God, let me out of here—did I say it? Or just think it? India wondered, and swallowed. But it's not too late now although it will be soon. I must have been *mad* to agree to this . . .

She closed her eyes and swallowed painfully again; not because she was feeling sick so much as scared stiff, and unbelievingly claustrophobic.

Then Giles's hand grasped one of hers firmly and she looked at him wide-eyed and he smiled and grimaced and she knew he knew exactly how she was feeling. A little sigh escaped her and she moved closer and rested her forehead on his shoulder, quite unwittingly. I can't help myself, she thought vaguely. It's comforting . . .

Then they were off the ground, hovering, turning, rising higher, and she couldn't help herself from lifting her head and looking out of the window to see the dark green hillside sliding by— and to discover it wasn't so terrifying after all. In fact it was quite fascinating.

Not that she could say she'd completely lost her sense of fear, but all the same . . .

'It was fantastic,' a glowing India Ballantyne was heard to say later that day.

They were back on Hamilton, having lunch at the Beach Bar with Brad and Petula. '. . . You can't believe how beautiful the reef is from the air! I wish I could describe it—but if you can imagine being thirty miles out to sea and you've left the islands behind you, and the water is very blue and deep-looking, and then you begin to see something quite different—patches of pink and sandy brown and white, and shallow lagoons of turquoise, clear, clear water—I just hope my photos turn out!'

'So you can recommend the Reef trip, India?' Brad enquired.

'I certainly can! And go by helicopter, I'm sure it's the best way. Now don't you laugh at me, Giles Ballantyne!' she warned with a grin.

'I wouldn't dream of it,' he responded perfectly seriously, but with his eyes alight with laughter. 'It's just that I've never seen anyone converted to anything so quickly or thoroughly.'

'And what did you do once you were there?' Petula asked.

'Well, you land on this pontoon—I closed my eyes for that bit. And then this—real character arrives with his glass-bottomed boat—he reminded me of a later day King Neptune, lots of hair although thinner, and he ferries you right up to where the reef starts. We had breakfast . . .'

'Breakfast? In a glass-bottomed boat?' Brad looked quizzical. 'How big was it?'

'Not big, and we had sandwiches and fruit,' India responded. 'It tasted marvellous!'

'Something about the Great Barrier Reef that generates a lot of enthusiasm!' Brad said wryly. 'Sandwiches!'

'Not everybody eats a horse for breakfast like you do,' Petula retorted. 'Go on, India.'

India bit into a succulent piece of pineapple that accompanied her ham steak. 'We got out and walked on the coral—I couldn't believe it. This great wall of living coral rising up from the depths and so many different varieties, and the colours! You'd go along treading on this quite dull-looking

coral and then come upon patches of the most
brilliant coloured stuff, pinks and oranges—some
of it really delicate—oh, and the clams! Have you
ever seen a live clam? Well, you know they have
those curved, serrated shells?' She demonstrated
with her hands. 'Inside they have . . . fleshy sort of
lips in the most unbelievable colours, sapphire
blue, emerald green striped with black . . .'

'Aren't they dangerous?'

'They can be if you get your finger or your foot
stuck in them,' Giles said. 'They shut up like a
clam.'

They all laughed. 'And the textures are so
different,' India went on. 'Some of the coral is soft
and slippery, some of it quite repulsive-looking
actually, but some so beautiful! Then we did some
snorkelling . . .' She stopped and sighed. 'I'll let
Giles tell you about that, I've run out of
superlatives. But the fish, so many colours again
and shapes and sizes—I could go back there
tomorrow! What's wrong?' she asked Giles,
suddenly aware that he was studying her medita-
tively from beneath half-closed lids.

'Wrong?' He smiled slightly. 'Nothing. It's just
that I don't think I've seen you looking so alive
and animated and beautiful before. Brad's right—
about the Reef.'

India looked fleetingly self-conscious, then had
to smile herself. 'It certainly got me in,' she
admitted ruefully. 'Coming home, we flew over
some of the islands and you could see the
cockatoos flying through the bush like big
butterflies, and we flew right over Hamilton and
got this fantastic bird's eye view of the place, and
we flew over Passage Peak—they can land up

there, believe it or not. But I'm not sorry they didn't today. I think that might have tried my spirit of adventurism too far.'

'I reckon we might try it tomorrow,' Brad said. 'What do you reckon, Pet?'

'I'm convinced,' Petula agreed enthusiastically.

They finished their lunch and India drained her wine glass and sat back, soaking up the sun.

'Any plans, anyone?' Brad queried.

'Not me,' India replied a little drowsily. 'I'm going to have a sleep . . .'

'I'm really tired,' she said to Giles as they climbed the last flight of stairs to their floor. 'Must be all the adventuring I've done today. What are you going to do now?' As she spoke she extracted her key from her holdall.

'I'm going to have a sleep too.' He took her key from her and opened her door. 'I didn't sleep very well, either, last night,' he added.

India had raised her hand to take her key back from him but it stopped in mid-air and her eyes flew to his to see that he was looking at her soberly, enquiringly.

She swallowed as she read the nature of that enquiry in his eyes, and felt a fine beading of sweat break out on her forehead, and something inside her said, *no*, I'm imagining things.

'India?' He said her name softly, almost flatly.

'I . . .' She licked her lips then took her key, 'Then I'll see you later,' she said huskily, and waited a little pointedly for him to step aside.

He did but something in his eyes mocked her briefly. 'All right,' he acquiesced, and turned away.

She closed the door behind her, but this time

instead of leaning back against it, stunned, she ran through and flung herself face down on the bed and shudders of disbelief, despair and torment wracked her slender body. I didn't fool him at all, she thought torturedly. Oh, what have I done . . .?

She must have fallen asleep unknowingly, because an hour or so later, she woke, feeling uncomfortable. She still had her swimsuit on under her clothes, but also a sense of dread pressed down on her like a living weight.

She lay for a while examining the ceiling bleakly, then she sighed and got up. What could one do? she wondered. Go home? *Ignore* it in the hope that it would go away, and hope he'd take the hint? Pretend she'd misread his eyes . . .?

'Perhaps I did,' she murmured. 'Only I'm twenty-five now, and I've seen that look in men's eyes often enough not to be naïve about it, surely?'

Oh, often! she thought bitterly. The kind of look that said—I could show you a thing or two your *old* husband wouldn't be up to . . . The kind of look that had left her feeling besmirched and angry. If only you knew, she'd sometimes longed to say.

Yet it hadn't been quite that in Giles's eyes, she mused. It had been something more direct, an acknowledgment that he'd read her mind and that it coincided with his.

'But it's impossible,' she whispered, fiddling unconsciously with her wedding ring. 'Not Giles . . .'

Why?

She looked around as the question slid across her mind, almost as if someone else had uttered it.

Why? Why is it impossible? It just *is*, she argued

with herself. Because of Rod—don't you see? We might have agreed to be friends, we could even achieve that possibly, but lovers—he'd always be there between us. And I don't want a lover and I don't suppose he could be contemplating marrying his father's widow. Oh *hell*, she thought intensely and stared out of the windows towards the sunlit beach, the sparkling sea, Passage Peak ... It's probably not even that easy to go home! Not direct, anyway, because there aren't daily flights direct to Hamilton from down south. You'd have to go to Proserpine or Mackay.

'And the explanations,' she muttered and gritted her teeth. 'I'm going home, Giles, because I've got the horrible feeling I might have fallen in love with you ... well, not in love precisely but *fallen* for you—no! I think I've got to just ignore it, put it out of my mind and heart, give it no chance to take any kind of root—let it wither and die at birth. That's what I've got to do. And in the meantime I'll go for a swim,' she said to herself, so ferociously that she had to laugh a little at herself.

It was Petula who joined India beside the pool, looking pretty in a pink bikini.

'This is your life,' she said happily, as she arranged her towel over a low lounger, and lay down beside India. 'Been in the water?'

'Yes, it's lovely!'

'Well, I have to confess I'm not a swimmer. I only like to dunk myself to cool off. Brad can't understand it!'

India grinned. 'Where is Brad?'

Petula glanced sideways at her. 'Playing tennis with Giles,' she said after the slightest hesitation.

'Rather Brad than me,' India replied with a grimace. But, she thought, there's no reason why I should be aware of Giles's every movement, is there? Unless . . .

But Petula interrupted her thoughts. 'I agree,' she said feelingly. 'In fact I'm so glad we've met up with you and Giles—they can do all the madly active things men like to do together, and leave us in a bit of peace. But they did say they'd be carting me—us, off for a swim in the sea after their game.'

India tensed inwardly. But there's nothing I can do, she reminded herself, other than play it cool.

Yet, she reflected, as she dressed for dinner that evening, she hadn't even had to do that. Giles did it for her . . . Well, not cool exactly, but as if nothing had ever happened between them—which it hadn't of course, but as if it had never crossed his mind. Maybe it didn't?

She stared at herself in the mirror, trying to concentrate and smoothing the wine-red dress she wore that tied on one shoulder and left the other bare.

But on the other hand, she mused, there was something lacking.

She narrowed her eyes and recalled Brad and Petula frolicking on the beach that afternoon. Petula had been determined not to swim, Brad equally determined she should, and the ensuing tussle had been very funny. India had laughed and so had Giles. Then he'd stood up rather abruptly and gone for a long swim out to the third pontoon by himself. And when he'd come back, he'd not addressed one remark to her personally, although she was possibly the only one to notice it.

It was just, she thought, an absence of the sort of warmth there was between us this morning on the Reef for example. She shivered suddenly and reached for her brush. She'd washed her hair and it floated in a dark gleaming cloud as the brush stroked through it. Her lips were painted wine-red to match her dress and she'd redone her nails to match. But all the time, as she'd prepared and dressed for dinner—the four of them had booked into the Dolphin Room—she'd been conscious of a dreadful feeling of nerves. At least with Brad and Petula, it would be easier; yet a lingering doubt stayed with her still. An apprehension that she was making an appalling mistake by not putting as much distance as she possibly could between herself and Giles Ballantyne, as soon as she possibly could.

Then he knocked on the door and she closed her eyes and drew a deep breath.

They said nothing to each other for a moment after she opened the door. He looked her up and down briefly and uncommunicatively and she felt her heart jolt once at the sight of him, with his tawny hair tamed and sleek, wearing a tan linen shirt and cream trousers.

And her lips parted under the sheer impact of his physcial presence and what it did to her—made her feel uncertain at the knees, shaky inside. I can't believe it! she thought dazedly.

He waited, expecting her to speak, she realised, and she shut her mouth with a click and turned faintly pink.

He lifted one eyebrow slightly then said drily, 'Ready?'

'Yes ... Yes, I am.' Only you shouldn't be,

India, a voice within said a little wildly. Plead a headache, go to bed, don't do this to yourself . . .

She said instead, 'I'll just get my purse.'

They walked in silence all the way to the Dolphin Room. Not that it was very far—across the bridge to the Beach Bar, across the suspension over the lighted pool, along the arcade past Lady Hamilton's and Lord Nelson's, through the coffee lounge, and then they were there in the tiered Dolphin Room, so named because there were actually dolphins frolicking in the deep pool right outside the windows, something that would have delighted India normally because she loved dolphins. But the silent walk had left her feeling drained and cold and hurt, she acknowledged ironically, and not in the mood to appreciate anything much. In fact it was a real effort to pin a smile on her face for Brad and Petula, already seated and looking happy and eager for their company.

To say that, by the time they'd eaten a superb and leisurely meal and spent a while over their coffee, India felt as if she'd been through a coffee grinder herself, was to put it mildly.

She'd talked and laughed and eaten and no one looking on would have suspected the effort it had cost her. But a feeling of strain about her temples had gathered momentum and was threatening to become a king-sized headache, a real one. And there was no one more relieved, inwardly, when Brad and Petula decided on an early night.

'What with the ravages of last night, not to mention three sets with my mate Giles, here,' Brad said ruefully, 'I do believe I'm ready for bed!'

'Glory be!' Petula rejoiced.

'I didn't say ready for sleep,' Brad murmured, with a wicked glint in his eye.

Petula lifted an eyebrow haughtily. 'Gentlemen should wait to be invited.'

'I might make you regret that remark,' Brad replied idly. 'I know just how to . . .'

'Brad!' Petula protested, blushing but laughing and with her eyes alight with affection. India turned away suddenly. They were so natural and so nice, she thought, this pair of lovers. Perhaps . . .

'Going to bed too, India?' Giles interrupted her thoughts as they all stood up, and she was quite sure she was not imagining the slightly sardonic note in his voice.

'I . . . no, I don't think so,' she managed to say lightly enough. 'I think I'll go for a walk along the beach first. Good night, all!' she added brightly and warmly, for Brad and Petula's sake, and walked away.

The beach was deserted and bright with moonlight that trailed a path of light across the water. She took off her high-heeled sandals and wandered down to the water's edge, then turned towards the rock pool and began to walk. I won't think, she promised herself. I'll just walk . . .

It wasn't that far to the as yet incompleted rock pool, but a young breeze had sprung up and it was refreshing. The band around her temples began to loosen. She turned back.

The buildings at this end of the beach were not completed either, and it was silent and very peaceful in the moonlight. A band of trees marked the limit of the beach and she wandered over to them, picking her way carefully, and she stopped there and leaned back against a twisted trunk with her face tilted upward, her arms hanging loosely at her sides, her purse in one hand, her shoes in the other. And she stared up at the dark sky and the millions of stars—and discovered that she'd never felt as lonely or bereft. And slow, silent tears welled and trickled down.

Then a shadow moved and she tensed and saw the gleam of reddish-brown hair in the light of the moon and all the stars. It was Giles.

She straightened in a queerly taut, defensive way and dashed at the tears on her cheek with the back of her hand. 'I . . .' She stopped.

'India,' his voice was deep and detached, his eyes unmercifully probing, 'why are you fighting this? Tell me.'

He moved closer so that she had to tilt her head slightly backwards. 'Why did you follow me?'

'That's no way to answer a question—with a question. That's,' he said barely audibly, 'evading the issue.'

'I don't,' she took a breath, 'really know what the issue is.'

He smiled—she saw his lips move slightly. 'All right, this,' he said, and lifted a hand to touch her hair, to slide his fingers through the cloud of dark curls and stroke the nape of her neck. She couldn't help herself, her head drooped forward at the mesmerising touch of those square-tipped fingers on that tender skin, awakening quivering ripples throughout her whole body.

She dropped her shoes.

They hit the ground with a soft plop that brought her back to some kind of reality. She stiffened and tilted her chin.

'And this,' he said, and slid his arms around her.

'No,' she whispered raggedly.

'Yes,' he said, and bent his head to kiss the corner of her mouth.

She tried to free herself and dropped her purse. 'I can't,' she gasped.

'Try it . . .'

'It's wrong!'

'It's not wrong. There's no reason on earth why it should be.'

'There is, there is,' she wept.

'Shut up, India,' he said tersely. 'It can't be wrong to feel like this, not if we both feel it.'

'I . . .'

'Don't talk.'

She took a despairing breath. 'I . . .'

'Kiss me,' he insisted very quietly. 'You must know how to do it.'

'Not you . . .'

'Yes, *me*. Like this . . .'

'Giles . . . oh God . . .'

His mouth covered hers, effectively blotting out any further protests, but in fact there were none. Only the dazed thought that slid across India's mind that she was submitting herself to the enemy, and willingly now—kissing him back with a sort of fervent urgency that she was simply not strong enough to resist. Moving within his arms to get closer to him because her body was invaded with the same sense of urgency, her pulses leaping and quivering with a flickering of desire, the intensity of which she'd never yet felt.

'Come,' he said at last, his lips leaving her mouth to slide along a devastating path down the side of her throat.

She tilted her head back and shivered with pleasure.

'India?'

'Yes . . .?' It was a bare thread of sound.

'We can't stay here all night.' He lifted his head at last and smiled slightly at the dazed, uncomprehending look in her hazel eyes. 'Your shoes . . .' He released and steadied her, and bent down.

'Oh!' Her hand went to her mouth guiltily. 'And my purse.'

'I've got it—no, I'll carry them. Come,' he said again, and put his free arm around her shoulders.

They walked side by side, slowly back along the beach. Once she rested her head on his shoulder, and he stopped walking and just held her to him. 'Giles,' she whispered, but found she couldn't go on.

He said nothing and they started to walk again.

Outside her room, she lent back against the wall while he opened her purse and got out her keys.

'You're always doing this.' Her words seemed to echo queerly and her eyes flew to his, frightened and confused. 'Giles . . .'

He stared at her searchingly, then looked away and after a moment, put the key into the door and opened it. 'Good night, India.'

She winced and the world felt as if it had gone very cold. ' . . . No,' she whispered and reached for his hand and raised it to her lips. 'Come in . . . please.' She trailed her lips across his palm.

He said with an effort, his fingers closing around hers, 'If I do, you must know what's going to happen.'

'I know,' she murmured, and turned with his hand still in hers, to walk across the doorstep.

She'd only left one lamp on in the far corner of the room and it sprang to light softly as Giles put the power key in, releasing her hand to do so. India stopped uncertainly, feeling like an actress in a play who didn't know her lines, and experienced that hollow feeling of fright again. What kind of words should there be said? she wondered. Something affectionate? Or teasing? *Something* . . . but she couldn't think of one. Perhaps she should offer him a cup of coffee or a drink . . .

She turned with her lips parted but he'd put down her shoes and purse and was right behind her so that she almost bumped into him. 'I . . . I don't know what to say,' she stammered. 'Would you like a drink?'

'No.' A flicker of amusement lit his grey eyes. 'Unless you would.'

'No.' She licked her lips.

'Then how about picking up where we left off?' he said softly, and took her into his arms very gently. 'Or even starting again, like this.' He kissed her hair and began to stroke the back of her neck as he'd done earlier.

She stood very still in his arms, afraid but at the same time in a queer way relieved, that what she'd felt on the beach might have been quenched in the awkwardness of the moment. Relieved because there *had* been a frightening quality to it. To surrender your will to anyone, she thought, like that, to seem to have no choice in the matter—and he had offered her one at the door—seemed to her, in a moment of rationality, enough to scare her stiff.

But I've burnt my boats now, she thought starkly.

'India?' He pushed her away slightly and gazed

down at her, and she couldn't hide the tension in her eyes and knew what he must be thinking. But she found she couldn't bear him to be thinking that about her, and she lowered her lashes and whispered, 'Could you kiss me, please?' But she shivered as she spoke and then found she couldn't stop.

He didn't kiss her. He simply held her back close to him, almost as if he understood. She hid her face in his shoulder unhappily.

They stood like that for an age until a gradual feeling of warmth stole over her, a sweet feeling of . . . relief? she wondered. Because he'd understood? She moved, but only to free a hand and place it on his arm just above his elbow. And that was the moment she realised that those fires hadn't been quenched at all, only been hidden beneath a welter of confusion and uncertainty. Because, as her palm rested on his skin, she knew in a blinding flash, what she really wanted to do—to touch him, feel him, slide her hands and lips over his body . . .

He said, 'I'll go now.'

'*No* . . .' She moved convulsively then slid her palm up his arm beneath the short sleeve of his shirt. 'No, I'm all right now,' she whispered. 'I . . . was being foolish.'

'It's not foolish to hold back from something you're going to regret, India.'

She lifted her face finally. 'You never know what you're going to regret really, do you?' she murmured. 'I just know I don't seem to be able to resist this. I feel . . . as if I'll die a little inside if you go now. I don't know what it means—just that I can't help it. Will you . . . would you kiss me now, Giles?'

It was a long, searching kiss that left her gasping and trembling in his arms, her arms wound round his neck, and she didn't loosen them when he picked her up and carried her to the bed.

He sat down with her and only then did she slacken her hold to slide her hands beneath the collar of his shirt, stopping to undo a couple of buttons.

He laughed softly and hugged her.

'Is something wrong?'

'Yes—I can't figure out how your dress undoes.'

'Oh . . .' She lifted her head and an impish smile lit her eyes. 'It's a trick dress. No, not really . . . it unties on the shoulder and there's a zip down the other side. Giles . . .' Her eyes sobered and she took her underlip between her teeth.

'What?' He looked at her, suddenly alert.

She flushed. 'Nothing—just felt a bit forward, I guess.' She glanced away uncomfortably.

'Look at me, India,' he said steadily. And when she did finally, still a little flushed, he continued, 'That wasn't being forward. In fact I doubt if there is such a thing between a man and a woman. There's only what pleases them. Would it please you for me to undo your dress?'

'Oh yes,' she said at last.

He did more. He took off her strapless bra and gazed at her breasts with a suddenly indrawn breath.

'Don't you like them?' she whispered involuntarily, and looked immediately horrified.

He smiled slightly. 'They're perfect—I never suspected. You don't . . . flaunt them.'

This was true. She never wore bikinis, and all her swimsuits had built-in bras and she never wore plunging necklines or tight tops.

'I used to worry that they were too big . . .'

'Too big,' he said huskily and bent his head forward to lay his cheek on them suddenly. 'No, they're beautiful, perfect . . .'

She trembled as his hands moved to push her dress down further and curved about her slender waist. Then his lips were moving on one nipple, kissing it, taking it between his teeth and tugging at it very gently.

She gasped and arched her body and crossed her hands over the back of his head, flooded with a primitive feeling of extreme sensuousness.

He did the same to the other nipple and she wanted to tell him to stop, that it was too much, but she didn't. She slid her fingers through his hair instead and tilted her head back with a queer little sound in her throat, a low moan of pleasure and anguish.

She thought later, as he made love to her with a sureness of touch that alternately took her breath away and released inhibitions that she hadn't known she possessed, that this must be someone else in Giles Ballantyne's arms, that this passionate person couldn't be her, not this shameless creature who cried out in joy and yearning and guided his hands, his lips, dug her nails into his back until she realised what she was doing with a gulp of contrition . . .

'Oh God, I'm *sorry* . . .'

'Don't be.'

'But . . .'

'I don't mind.'

She wanted to say that he must, that she didn't know what possessed her, only their bodies seemed as one, moving towards a pinnacle so intense she couldn't speak, she couldn't think, she could only move beneath him . . .

It was like nothing she'd ever known, that pinnacle. So much so that she felt her mind slipping away as her body was racked with exquisite shudders of it, slipping away into some dark, dizzy place . . . with one vague thought in it. How could it be so different . . .?

CHAPTER SIX

HER eyelids fluttered open and she moved uncertainly. She was lying in someone's arms, she was naked and totally disorientated. Then it all came flooding back as she stared up into Giles's concerned grey eyes.

'India? Are you all right?'

'Oh—yes,' she said with difficulty. 'Yes I am ...'

'Do you always faint, then?' he asked a little drily.

'No! Did I? I ... I don't know why. How long?'

'Only a few seconds, but long enough to give me the fright of my life. I thought I must have hurt you.'

She licked her lips. 'No, you didn't ... No. It was so ...' She stopped, remembering how it had been, and a delicate colour tinged her cheeks.

'So?' he prompted and smoothed her hair.

She turned her face into his shoulder, feeling too hot and shaken to speak.

'It was—incredible for me,' he said very quietly. 'Like nothing else I've known. India?' He tipped her face up and dropped a light kiss on her temple.

'Yes,' she whispered, 'it was for me too.' But there was something troubled in her eyes that she couldn't hide.

'What is it?' He traced the outline of her mouth.

'I ...' What *is* it? she wondered. I'm not too sure myself ... 'I feel a bit of a fool, fainting like that. And ... oh!' Her eyes dilated. 'Your back ...'

A smile lit his eyes. 'If that's all you're worried about, forget it. I don't suppose you're entirely unmarked either. Anyway, I enjoyed it. Would you like something? To drink?'

'I don't think I feel like anything but sleeping. Will you,' she hesitated, 'go back to your room?'

'Do you want me to?'

She hesitated again. 'No,' she whispered finally, and gripped his hand.

'Then I won't. Here,' he eased her away so that she was lying on the bed, not in his arms but very close, 'how's that?' He picked up her hand again.

'Fine,' she responded huskily and moved her cheek on the pillow, conscious that she didn't even have the energy to move her limbs. But in the moment or two before she fell asleep, that insidious thought slid through her mind again— how could it be so different?

She struggled up through layers of sleep because someone was saying her name and touching her hair. 'Yes, Rod,' she mumbled sleepily. Then her eyes flew open and it was Giles with his hand arrested on her hair.

They stared at each other, he with his grey eyes narrowed and probing.

'I'm sorry,' she whispered, appalled.

Something flickered in his eyes that she couldn't read. 'Forget it,' he advised. 'Are you all right?'

She struggled to sit up, pulling the sheet up as she did so and she gazed around a little bemusedly. 'Yes. What time is it? You're ... already dressed.'

'Actually, it's not that late—about a quarter to nine. And the only reason I'm dressed,' he said with a glint of humour in his eyes, 'is because the architect and the surveyor are arriving in about half-an-hour's time from Proserpine, and I've hired a boat to go over to the island.'

'Oh, I forgot, it's Wednesday,' she said guiltily. 'Half an hour? I . . .' She lay back against the pillow a little helplessly.

'You don't have to come—not today,' he reassured, and picked up her hand. 'We've got three more days. You could—relax.'

'W-would you mind?'

'No. So long as you're okay.'

'I am, really. Just . . .' she grimaced ruefully, 'slow off the mark.'

He smiled. 'Don't be fooled into thinking I don't feel that way too. In fact I could think of nothing I'd rather be doing than spending a long, lazy, slow off-the-mark day with you—preferably doing this from time to time, very slowly.' He uncurled her fingers from about the sheet and pulled it down.

She caught her breath as he cupped her breasts and stroked her nipples with a featherlight touch of his thumbs. 'I can't believe you worried about them,' he said, in a curiously husky voice.

'Girls . . . worry about strange things, I suppose,' she answered raggedly and slid her fingers through his hair because she couldn't help herself.

'Well,' he said after a moment, 'enough of this.' But he turned his head and kissed the underside of her upraised arm, and she shivered with pleasure.

'I thought you said . . .'

'I did,' he cut in, 'and I'm about to be very stern with myself.' He transferred his lips to hers and kissed her tenderly. 'Right now.' He pulled up the sheet and stood up. 'You'll never know how stern,' he added with a grin. 'I don't know what time I'll be back. Don't go away, will you?'

'I won't,' she promised. 'Why ... did you say that?'

For a second it was as if a shadow crossed his eyes. Then it was gone and he shrugged. 'No reason. Breakfast's on until ten, by the way. See you later.' He picked up her hand and kissed it lightly, and was gone.

She heard the door close softly and turned on to her side and slid her arm beneath the pillow. And stayed that way for about ten minutes, staring at nothing in particular. Then she got up slowly and took a long, warm shower. She was marked too, she discovered as she blotted the moisture from her body with a thick cream towel. There was a pattern of faint bruises on her upper arm, and her breasts felt heavy and tender. She closed her eyes for a moment and stood with the towel pressed to her mouth, remembering and feeling weak at the pit of her stomach.

She had fruit juice, some stewed plums, toast and tea for breakfast, and had looked around a little warily for Brad and Petula, before re-membering that they'd gone to the Reef.

The tide was out, which meant most people were concentrated around the pool so she walked down the few steps to the beach, found a lounger which she pulled under the thatched umbrella for shade, settled herself comfortably and reached into her straw holdall for her sketch pad.

The sky was perfectly clear and the sunlight was dancing on the water further out. And far out the bulk of other islands was tinted purplish blue as they rose out of the glittering water.

She gripped her pencil and sketched and after a while, Passage Peak was distinguishable, then One Tree Hill and Catseye Beach . . .

It was a quarter to twelve when she looked at her watch and blinked. She hadn't realised how the time had passed. She looked down at her sketch pad but unseeingly, and her pencil moved and a man's head began to take shape in one corner—Giles. Her pencil hovered about the rough drawing, and then she sat up abruptly and closed the book with a click and dropped it into her holdall. And she gathered up her stuff and decided to go for a swim in the pool.

Refreshed and revived, she ordered toasted cheese sandwiches for lunch at the Beach Bar and a pineapple juice and sat in the sun on the verandah, surrounded by happy, chattering people. But even with her hat on she soon grew hot and drowsy, in an entirely pleasant and lazy way that made the cool tiles of her room and the wide smooth bed seem infinitely inviting.

The tide was well in when she woke and over her cream terrace wall, she could smell the heat of the still, blinding afternoon. The leaves of the gum trees shimmered with it around the pointed green roofs of the *bures*. All the same there were people sunbaking on the beach, and sailing the catamarans and windsurfers and there was a boat operating paraflying trips.

India watched someone take off in some

wonderment, knowing that this was something she would never be converted to.

She stayed on watching the bright parachute circling beyond the lagoon and wondered what the man up there was feeling. Like a bird? I hope he's not as timid about these things as I am, she mused. The other thing is, he'd got to get down again!

But the descent was accomplished unbelievably smoothly. As the boat headed towards the beach in a curving run and reduced speed, the parachute floated downwards and the man landed in the shallows so gently he didn't even stumble. She shook her head in amazement and contemplated going for a swim in that clear inviting sea but decided to wait a while. It was really too hot to be out in the sun, even in the water where you burnt so easily.

And she spent the next hour rinsing out some undies and tidying up her clothes and things. She made herself a cup of tea and wondered when Giles would be back. When she found herself wondering this for the fourth time she shook herself mentally, and went for that swim.

She swam out to the third pontoon and climbed up for a rest. It was further than it looked, but when she got her breath back, she felt stimulated and alive. The swim back to the beach completed her feeling of well-being and she lazed in the shallows for a while, reluctant to leave the magic of the water, and finally found herself surrounded by an assortment of little children in the charge of the resort nanny, and with a beach attendant on hand to help out as the children took to the water with shrieks of delight—or was it because the nanny was young and very pretty? she wondered.

He was rather like a young, bronzed Greek god, and she fell to thinking that it would be a great job to be on an island like this. Especially if you were into water sports—the beach attendants supervised all the craft that you could take on to the water, gave sailing lessons if needed, and snorkelling and scuba diving classes and were always at the ready with their rubber dinghy with its high-powered motor if you got into trouble out there.

She guessed it would be about five-thirty at last, and decided to go back to her room to wait, although she could have joined Brad and Petula whom she spied with a noisy group of people about the pool But India felt oddly shy about meeting them, and was conscious of a growing feeling of tension and constraint too.

So preoccupied was she that when a hand tapped her on the shoulder as she was climbing the steps to her room, she jumped about a foot.

'Going my way, ma'am?'

She turned. 'Oh, Giles! It's you. You gave me a fright!'

'I thought you looked very deep in thought.' He smiled down at her and took her hand.

India felt her heart turn over and her pulses start to beat erratically, and her lips quivered because she felt like saying a little desperately, I *missed* you. But she asked instead, 'How was your day?'

'Great! I'll tell you about it. But at the moment I'm dying of thirst. Feel like offering me a beer?'

'Of course . . .'

In her room she handed him a frosty cold can from the fridge and poured herself a sparkling glass of mineral water. 'Do you want a glass?'

'No.' He tilted the can to his lips. 'It tastes just great like this,' he added with a grin. 'How was your day?'

'Lovely,' she said lightly. 'Apart from swimming I did nothing. In fact I might just get out of my wet togs if you'll excuse me for a moment. Then I can sit down.'

She walked into the bathroom and the swinging louvred doors closed behind her. She pulled off her blouse and untied the straps of her costume behind her neck and in the mirror saw the doors swing open.

She turned to face him, her eyes wide and wary.

'You don't have to hide away to do this, surely,' he said quietly, his grey eyes flickering over her from head to toe.

'No ... no I don't, I suppose,' she answered barely audibly and looked away. 'I wasn't trying to hide, precisely.'

'I'm glad,' he commented. 'Then you won't mind if I do it for you.'

It wasn't a question, it was an assumption and she didn't, couldn't deny it, as he slowly stripped her wet swimsuit from her body and she stepped out of it. Nor could she stop herself from moving into his arms and revelling in the feel of his hands on her damp, cool skin. This is what I was waiting for, she thought dimly as she wound her arms around his neck and sought his lips, and what I was afraid of at the same time. How queer ... to be so confused.

A little later, when he said, 'Come ...' as she was sliding her lips along the smooth skin of his shoulders where she'd pushed his shirt away, her eyelashes flew up and she found she was staring at herself in the mirror and barely recognising herself because her eyes were brilliant and a little unfocused, her lips trembling with desire. She closed her eyes on this wanton, voluptuous creature as they moved apart and Giles took her hand to lead her to the bed.

Not that closing her eyes solved anything. Their love-making was as momentuous as it had been the night before, better even because of an intimate, lovely feeling of knowing, of having been there before.

She didn't faint this time. She lay quivering in his arms for a long time afterwards, though, as the sun set and twilight descended.

'I've been thinking about this all day,' he said at last and moved his chin on her hair.

'So have I . . .' In one way or another, an inner voice added.

'What would you like to do this evening?'

'Nothing,' she murmured against his shoulder and felt him laugh silently.

'I mean——' she freed herself with a rueful little smile.

'I know what you mean.' He curved a hand around the back of her neck, beneath her hair and drew her back against him. 'Something quiet and just the two of us.'

'Yes,' she whispered.

'Then I think I might have the answer. There's a cabaret on tonight over here, which means Mariners' might be a quiet spot to go for a meal a bit later and even a spot of quiet dancing. How does that sound?'

'Perfect . . . What about the architect and the surveyor?'

'They've gone back . . . hang on.' He kissed her hair and got up to get another beer. 'Want something?'

'No.' She flushed faintly because she'd been unable not to watch the easy grace and power of his naked body. If he noticed her discomfort, he said nothing. In fact he glanced out of the sliding glass doors that led to the terrace and frowned. Then he reached for a towel and wrapped it round his hips and stepped outside. A moment later he came back in and looked around and picked up her fluffy yellow bathrobe which had been laid across the bottom of the bed. 'Come and look at this,' he suggested softly, handing it to her.

It was that not-quite-dark period although the sun had set, and he pointed upwards. India gazed at the sapphire blue sky and drew a breath suddenly. 'What are they?'

'Flying foxes. Thousands of them . . . I've never seen so many.'

She stared upwards, entranced as wave upon wave of the ghostly black creatures flitted across the sky silently. Then gradually it got too dark to see them.

'That was fantastic,' she said. 'So many!'

'Even if they were circling, it was a multitude. Coming back to bed?'

'Mmm . . .'

'What were we talking about?' he asked, as they lay back against the pillows comfortably. India still had her robe on and her knees drawn up, so that she was curled up close to his side.

'The island—the architect and the surveyor, actually.'

'Yes. Well, the architect's gone back to Brisbane

to come up with some rough concepts and the surveyor will be organising a proper survey which will take some time. Until then, and until we come up with a—theme, we can't really do much.'

'Did you get any ideas? Today?' she asked.

He was silent for a time then he looked at her with a smile at the back of his eyes. 'No. I was a little distracted, as a matter of fact.' She coloured faintly and he touched her cheek. 'Why do you do that? I love it, incidentally, so don't stop.'

'I always have. It's a great disability. It makes you feel—transparent.'

'But in this instance, why? Shouldn't I have thought about you today?'

She bit her underlip and wondered how to explain that she'd always had a certain shy reserve about anything to do with sex, despite or perhaps because of her mother's liberated views on the subject. Or perhaps it was just the way she was made. Only how *to* explain that, in view of the way she'd acted and responded over the last two days? He'd have to find it hard to believe . . .

'No, there's no reason for you not to have,' she said. 'I . . . it's just something I do,' she added helplessly.

'All right,' he answered idly, and stroked her hair. 'One thing I did notice, being particularly alive to it at the moment, is how beautiful it is. It's smaller than Hamilton but not as small as Daydream . . .'

She listened, relaxing again and finding herself fascinated as he described the secluded beaches and bays, the bird-filled bush, the point on the island where you gaze around at the Whitsundays in their glory.

'It sounds,' she said dreamily at last, and stopped abruptly.

'Go on,' he prompted.

She grimaced. 'I was going to say it sounds too beautiful to share with other people. I mean, that it would be a nice place to live . . .'

'Strange you should say that, but the thought crossed my mind.'

'Very uncommercial and unprofessional of us,' she remarked with a wry smile.

'Very exclusive, too—to want to shut the public out of all this beauty.'

India hesitated then said, 'I was thinking about that on the helicopter flight. Part of the magic of the Whitsundays is the fact that there are still deserted, tropical islands left, don't you think? I mean, this is a marvellous place for a holiday, but it would be a pity if there were no undeveloped islands left.'

'Sounds as if you have the same instincts I once had,' he replied with a tinge of self-mockery and irony.

She tilted her face upwards. 'What do you mean?'

'In my university days, I was something of a greenie.'

She stared at him, her eyes wide with wonder.

He laughed. 'What's so strange about that?'

'Nothing,' she said hastily.

'But you find it hard to believe?'

'Well, I wouldn't have suspected it,' she confessed honestly. 'But then I've only ever seen the dynamic, forceful businessman side of you, I guess.' She tailed off and flushed brilliantly at the way he was looking at her. 'I—I mean,' she stuttered, 'well, we don't know each other very well, do we?'

His eyelids lowered briefly then it was a piercingly direct, grey glance he shot at her. 'Are you trying to say we've put the cart before the horse, India?'

'I ... no, I don't really know,' she answered confusedly. 'Anyway, it just ... happened, didn't it?'

'We could talk about the way it "just" happened if you'd like to,' he said quietly.

'I ... don't think I could find the right words,' she whispered finally, looking down.

He fiddled with a strand of her hair for a while and she waited and wondered, a little fearfully, what he was going to say next ...

'Then should we stop being incredibly lazy and get dressed and walk over to Mariners' for the evening, where we could continue the process of getting to know each other?'

Her lashes flew up and she saw that he was not quite smiling at her, with an expression of mingled amusement and affection.

'Oh, yes,' she breathed, a curious sensation of relief flooding her.

He kissed her forehead. 'So be it.'

She'd donned a pair of snowy white cotton slacks and a knitted top with short puffed sleeves in bands of cinnamon and white, and a pair of flat, white shoes in deference to the informality of Mariners'.

She and Giles were among the very few patrons when they were ushered into one of the banquette tables with its high-backed, insulating chairs. Not that you were really insulated or isolated from the dance floor or the bar or the other tables, only your immediate neighbours.

But by the time they'd finished their meal, more people had drifted in and some were dancing but to a much quieter beat than that of two nights ago.

They hadn't talked much, but not because of any feeling of constraint. In fact India had discovered with some surprise that she felt oddly peaceful and content. And when he asked her to dance, she got up willingly and a little dreamily.

They danced for a long time as the floor gradually filled up, again not talking much—it seemed unnecessary as their bodies moved in perfect unison. But finally he brought her to a stop and she rested her forehead on his shoulder for a moment or two, unwilling to leave the haven of his arms. Then she looked up at him with something of what she was feeling etched clearly in her eyes and he held her very close and said huskily, 'Don't look at me like that unless you want to be kissed very thoroughly, and publicly'

She caught her bottom lip between her teeth, then found herself smiling a little teasingly, 'All right, I won't.' And she directed a grave stare over his shoulder.

She felt him laughing silently then his lips descended on hers briefly and imperatively. 'That'll teach you,' he murmured wickedly, as she looked around them, a little flushed. But no one seemed to be taking the slightest notice of them, in fact everyone was dancing around them as if it was a perfectly natural occurrence, and they laughed together softly.

'Would you like a drink? A nightcap?' Giles queried, letting her go.

'I'd love a cup of coffee—will you excuse me for a moment?'

'Sure—it's over there.'

There was no-one in the powder room but as India was washing her hands a plump, elderly lady with a kindly face came in and said immediately, 'Oh there you are, Mrs Ballantyne! I thought you'd gone. You might not remember me, but I met you once a couple of years ago. My husband Bill was a business associate of your husband Rod.'

India stared at her as she rambled on, detailing when and where they'd met, and gradually a misty sort of recollection came back.

'Of course,' she said. 'Mrs . . .'

'Bingle,' the lady said happily, 'Bill and Dolly Bingle. I recognised you as soon as I came in and I said to Bill—why, there's that gorgeous Mrs Ballantyne. He recognised you straight off, too!'

India smiled embarrassedly and ruefully. 'I'm sorry, but I didn't see you.'

'You were dancing, luv,' Dolly Bingle said with a laugh. 'We haven't been here that long, and we're at one of those tables against the window— the closed in ones.'

'Oh, yes, so are we,' India murmured, and added after a moment, 'how long are you staying? Do you like it?'

'Couldn't say yet,' Dolly replied cheerfully. 'Our flight from Brisbane was delayed, so we've barely had a chance to catch our breath, let alone see much—anyway it was almost dark. That's why we're eating so late!' she added ingeniously.

'I'm sure you'll love it,' India replied warmly. 'I have.'

'Oh, I am glad! You know,' Dolly Bingle said, '*I* felt very sorry for you when I heard Rod had died—you two were so obviously in love it was beautiful to see. And *I* could see it. But I'd be the last person to say you have to spend the rest of your life mourning him. And don't you let anyone else tell you that. You just tell them to mind their own business!' she added with a comical look of fierceness that sat oddly on her plump, kindly face. 'I don't hold with that kind of nonsense, and so I told . . .'

She broke off and bit her lip and then to India's further surprise—her lips had parted and her eyes widened at this rambling and somewhat obscure monologue—Dolly Bingle hugged her briefly but warmly and said, 'There now, you go back to your young man, and I better go somewhere before I burst! Might see you on the beach tomorrow! 'Bye now . . .'

India left the powder room slowly, her mind reeling slightly under a succession of images . . . Rod's principally. How could someone she barely knew, bring him back to mind so vividly, she wondered, so that it was like a blow to her heart? How could I have *forgotten*?

She glanced around then as if she'd forgotten where she was. And the first person her gaze came to rest upon was Bill Bingle, perhaps because he was looking rather fixedly at the powder-room door.

India blinked and found herself remembering him completely—a thin, rather pompous little man, fond of the sound of his own voice, Rod used to say . . .

All the same, she smiled and lifted a hand in his

direction—and in a flash of understanding that came like a sunburst in its clarity, discovered that the obscurities of Dolly Bingle's speech were no longer so obscure.

For Bill Bingle returned her smile as freely and willingly as a man ordered to do so at gunpoint, raised his hand limply and turned away abruptly.

. . . I don't hold with that kind of nonsense and so I told . . . so I told Bill? India thought incredulously, then with sudden certainty. They were arguing about me. They saw me dancing with Giles and I can just *hear* Bill Bingle saying something like—*Told you so. Told you she only married Rod Ballantyne for his money. Why, it's barely a year since he died . . . and look at her!*

'India . . .?'

She blinked and realised that Giles was standing in front of her. 'Oh . . .' She swallowed.

'Something wrong?'

'No.' Pride—it had to be something like that—helped her to smile up at him and say lightly, 'I'm looking forward to my coffee.'

He eyed her narrowly for a moment then took her hand and they walked back to their table.

And was it pride, she wondered, that helped her to act perfectly normally for the next ten minutes? A sort of defiance that kept at bay the dark forces gathering within her? Anyway, whatever effect it was having on Mr Bill Bingle, who can't even see it, it's fooling Giles, she thought ironically.

'Had enough?' he asked.

'Mmm.'

'Want to walk back or take a taxi?'

She thought, a taxi—no, we'll get back too soon. Before I've had a chance to *think*. Yet . . .

'India?'

'Walk, I think. The exercise will do me good.'

But there was an unpleasant surprise awaiting them at Mango Tree Corner, as India thought of it. They'd crossed the road at the summit of the hill and only by accident weren't holding hands—she'd bent down to shake a stone out of her shoe when a figure loomed up before them, and Lance Kidder said, 'Well! I'd given up hope of tracking you two down tonight. Giles, India, how are you?'

'What the hell are you doing here, Lance?' Giles demanded after a moment, and not entirely pleasantly, India thought. She herself had gasped in surprise.

Lance Kidder smiled mockingly. 'No reason I *shouldn't* be here, is there?' he drawled, but there was something slyly insinuating in his eyes as he scanned them both that caused India to catch her breath. Did he think he'd caught them . . . doing what? she wondered. Oh God, exactly what were they doing . . .?

'I meant,' Giles said impatiently, 'what made you decide to come out of the blue like this?'

'Oh, one or two things. Decided I ought to see things for myself seeing as we're committed to this resort. I'm sure it's a pleasant way of . . . doing things.' His tone was outright mocking and his eyes slid over India in a way that made her shiver inwardly. But before Giles could say anything he went on, 'And to apprise you, my dear Giles, of something rather electrifying.'

Giles frowned. 'Like what?' he asked curtly.

'That take-over bid. It seems you were right to be concerned,' Lance Kidder murmured. 'There have been some significant share movements in the last few days, old son. Thought you'd like to know. I had planned on being here earlier today, but the flight was delayed, unfortunately, and by the time I got to my room you weren't contactable. But I was sure I'd bump into you—and India, some time this evening,' he said with unmistakable satire.

Why? The question slid across India's mind. He *wanted* to catch them in compromising circumstances and he had been pretty sure he would. Why? I don't understand what's going on ... he must know we hate each other, Giles and I ... She closed her eyes briefly. Had hated each other, rather. But Lance couldn't possibly know how things have ... changed. So why ...?

Giles cut through her thoughts, his voice clipped and businesslike. 'Where are you staying?'

'Allamanda—the same building you and India are in,' Lance Kidder replied.

'Then if you've eaten, I suggest we go back there and talk business.'

They walked the rest of the way in silence, but of the three of them only Kidder seemed to be relaxed and at ease. Giles wore a slight frown and India decided his thoughts had switched completely to business. Which puzzled her and hurt her a little, but pleased her too, she discovered in some despair. Puzzled her because she couldn't help wondering if she'd imagined Lance Kidder's insinuations, hurt that he could have suddenly put her out of mind so completely, yet pleased because if he'd so much as taken her hand it would have given Kidder the proof he seemed so avidly to be seeking. Or *had* she imagined it?

Then they were outside her door and Giles said,

'You're a director, India. Do you want to come along and be in this?'

She licked her lips. 'I . . . I think I'm too tired for it tonight. Besides, I'm not really a business-woman—as we all know. I couldn't contribute much. Perhaps you could tell me about it tomorrow.'

Giles stared down at her, his grey eyes indecipherable. Then he said, 'All right,' and bent his head to kiss her on the lips. 'Sleep well,' he added almost beneath his breath, and touched her face lightly.

India caught her breath as he turned away, having proclaimed for all the world to see how things stood between them, and she caught Lance Kidder's eyes blazing unmistakably with insolent triumph before he too turned away.

In her room she sank on to the bed and stared unseeingly in front of her. This—on top of Bill and Dolly Bingle! she thought dazedly. I can't stand it—more to the point. I don't *under*stand it, not any of it.

She buried her face in her hands and when she lifted it finally, it was flushed and tear-streaked and her hazel eyes were bleak.

She waited a moment then reached for the telephone. She spoke into it, waited a couple of minutes, spoke into it again, gratefully, and put it down.

Then she stood up, found her sketchpad and tore a sheet off it and wrote a note. And then she started to pack.

CHAPTER SEVEN

LATE the next afternoon India unlocked the door of her unit in Surfers' with a mingled sigh of relief and exhaustion.

As she locked the door behind her it was like entering a haven of peace and security—a fortress where those dark forces within her and without lost their terrifying power.

She left her bag in the entrance hall and wandered across the turquoise carpet to stand beside the Abbot's chair touching the silk, outlining with her finger the griffins and the birds woven into it. Then she sat down in it, her head back, her hands in her lap and felt the day loosening its grip on her.

Beautiful Hamilton Island had never been so beautiful as she'd sailed away from it very early that morning. They'd been incredibly helpful when she'd rung Reception the night before and explained that for urgent personal reasons she had to get back to Brisbane as soon as possible. There was no direct flight back the next day, the girl had explained but an early boat leaving for Shute Harbour would give her the opportunity of transporting via Airlie Beach to Proserpine to catch a flight from there.

And so India had been up at five-thirty and ready when a mini-bus had called for her and her luggage and she'd left openly, only asking her bus driver to deliver a note back to Reception for Giles Ballantyne.

But she hadn't expected the wrench to her heart as the boat sailed out of Hamilton Harbour and not only because it all looked so beautiful, but because of the fact that she was running away without having the courage to face Giles.

The rest of the day had been a blur of coaches and aircraft, another coach down to the Gold Coast, a taxi home, but at least it had given her the opportunity to think.

'Which I don't seem to be able to do too well when I'm with him,' she said out aloud and laid her cheek on the silk panel on the side of the chair. 'To sort some things out with myself so that at least, if he comes, I can explain. If he comes . . .'

He came, three days later.

Three days during which India had achieved a composure of spirit and even decided he would not come. He wouldn't be able to forgive her for leaving like that, for what she'd said in the note she'd left—*I find I can't forget your father . . .*

But she discovered herself tensing when the doorbell rang that afternoon, for she rarely received visitors and for a blinding instant wishing it was Giles, then going hot and cold with fear in case it was.

But she steadied herself and stared at the Abbot's chair for a moment, then went to answer the door.

'Hello, Giles,' she said quietly.

He stared at her, his mouth in a hard line, his expression contemptuously sardonic, as if to say—I don't believe you, India.

She flushed and looked away, consumed with

guilt, and wondered hollowly how well her explanations and intentions would stand up against his physical presence. But they *had* to, she reminded herself.

She said, 'Come in. Would you like a drink?'

He followed her through to the lounge and spoke for the first time. 'Thanks.'

She poured him a Scotch and water and on an impulse, one for herself. She hesitated because he was still standing, then carried his drink over to him. But he didn't accept it, just stood looking down at her with his hands shoved into his trouser pockets, his eyes hard and mocking.

He wore the same suit he'd had on for the board meeting, one part of her mind observed, but with a blue-and-white striped shirt. He looked tired too, as he had *that* afternoon, but nonetheless something in his eyes frightened her.

She half-turned away to put his drink down on the glass-topped table, but as she straightened he moved abruptly and caught her wrist.

Her eyes flew to his and she said his name on a breath and tried to pull free. But he only smiled coldly and pulled her into his arms.

'Dear India,' he said softly but menacingly so that she shivered in spite of herself, 'there are some things you can't turn the clock back on. Oh,' he added through his teeth, 'you can run away, you can make excuses, but there's one thing you can't change. This . . .'

It was a long, forceful kiss he subjected her to. At least that's how it started out. She tried to wrench her mouth away but he was far too clever for her. He lifted his head immediately and looked at her ironically, and tears of despair pricked her eyelids because she knew that he knew she was fighting herself as much as him.

That was when she sagged against him, momentarily defeated and he took ruthless advantage of it. He started to kiss her again, but she had not the will left to fight.

'Do you see what I mean?' he asked at last, still holding her in his arms.

She closed her eyes.

'India?' he prompted.

She opened her eyes at last and they were full of tears. 'It doesn't change things . . .'

'It *must*,' he said, and the look in his eyes was as violent as the barely suppressed savagery of his words. 'Look,' his mouth compressed into that hard line then he sighed briefly and continued less abrasively, 'we became lovers because it was what we both wanted. Isn't that true, India?' His eyes challenged her.

She nodded after a moment. 'But . . .'

'You did want it, didn't you?' he cut in.

'All right!' She pulled herself free and he let her go. She turned away with her head bowed then swung back to face him. 'Yes, I wanted it,' she said in a low intense voice. 'But that doesn't mean I . . . understand it. Who's to say I'm not just a lonely widow? Who's to say any reasonably attractive man couldn't have . . . made me want it? Who's to say they're not all right? The Lance Kidders and the Bingles, and you yourself, Giles . . .'

'Who the hell are the Bingles?' he interrupted.

'It doesn't matter.'

'Yes, it does. Tell me,' he commanded.

She told him, angrily, and his eyes narrowed in

recollection. 'I thought something had happened. Why didn't you tell me then?'

'Why? I don't know,' she said with an effort. 'It's not important.'

'Precisely.' His voice was grim and his eyes mocking. 'So why did you let it get to you?'

'I *meant*,' she said drily, 'that Dolly and Bill Bingle aren't important, but their reactions were. They made me stop and think . . .'

'It seems everyone and his dog has the power to make you do that, India, except me.'

She stared at him frustratedly. 'Giles . . . look, just let me get back to what I was saying.'

'Something about any reasonably attractive man?'

'*Yes*. And I was about to remind you that you yourself said to me once—you actually said to me—"Give it . . . a few years, India, and you'll find yourself eyeing younger men, I'd like to bet." Do you remember saying that to me?'

A muscle moved in his jaw, but she went on, her eyes glittering, 'I can't help wondering if this isn't some form of revenge on your part.'

'So it's still that bothering you?'

'It's not *only* that,' she retorted. 'But why shouldn't it? That wasn't the only unpleasant thing you ever said to me—in fact it was quite mild compared to some of them. And now this, out of the blue! I . . .'

'What else bothers you, then?' he interrupted.

She took a breath. 'The way Lance Kidder—and he's not the only one—but the way his knowing looks and veiled sneers degrade everything that was between Rod and me. Drag it through the mire until,' her voice dropped, 'I even begin to have doubts about it myself. Which is crazy, because I know I loved Rod ... that I'd give anything to have him back.'

She dropped her head into her hands and just stood there helplessly.

Some moments later Giles said, 'Here ...'

She lifted her head and saw that he was offering her her drink. She took it after a moment and he said, 'Sit down,' and guided her to the settee. She sank down and sipped the Scotch.

He picked up his own drink but didn't sit down himself. Instead he stared at the painting of the ghost gums for a time. Then he said, 'Let's talk about sex,' and looked at her at last.

She tensed visibly. 'W-what do you mean?'

'Isn't that an area where your doubts creep in?' he queried, and she sucked in a distraught breath.

'How ...?' She stopped abruptly.

'Did I know?' he finished for her, and smiled slightly but not with any amusement. 'For several reasons. You seemed to be so astonished and bemused, so uncertain afterwards, as if it was something that had never happened to you before, almost guilty. Then there was the curious fact that you fainted the first time. I suppose I could congratulate myself about that,' he said ironically, 'only I don't usually make women faint, nor do I have the desire to, I find. So I gathered there had to be something ... that it had been very different for you.'

She looked away as a bright wave of colour stained her cheeks. 'I can't talk about it,' she said in a suffocated voice, at last.

'My dear,' he said very levelly, 'if you think I want to pry and probe into my father's love life, you're mistaken. All I'm interested in is the bearing it has on our admittedly very brief, but all the same intensely passionate love life. Because I think that might be one of the reasons you're tormented by so many doubts, why you're determined to write yourself off as a lonely widow ready to fall into the arms of the first man who came along—leaving aside, for the moment, the irony that they happened to be *my* arms.'

'It's all part of . . .'

'Don't kid yourself, India,' he said mockingly. 'What we had was something on its own. We affected each other deeply, and if you don't believe that go out and fall into the arms of the very next reasonably attractive man you meet.'

She flinched.

'That doesn't appeal to you?' he demanded cruelly.

She paled and a flicker of anger sparked in her eyes. *'No!'*

'Then let's talk—no, you're right,' he added, as if reading her mind. 'Not here.' He looked at his watch. 'I'll take you out to dinner.'

'I couldn't eat—I'm not hungry.'

'Then we'll go for a drive.'

'I . . .'

'You don't have to change or anything,' he said impatiently as she glanced down at her simple tangerine cotton shift and lime-green sandals. 'You look beautiful—you always do,' he finished harshly, as if it angered him and hurt him in a queer way.

India hesitated, puzzled for a moment and suddenly thinking of him and not herself. After all, she had gone to bed with him willingly, and been deeply affected by him. But she'd assumed a little blindly that the torment was all one-sided. Yet that odd note in his voice made her wonder . . .

'All right.' She stood up.

They drove north, silently and aimlessly, she thought. Past the Brisbane turn-off and through Angler's Paradise and Runaway Bay towards Paradise Point. But when they'd gone as far as they could along the Point, Giles turned the car round and stopped beside a long stretch of park fringing a beach. She thought that he must have known where he was going all the time, because it was a beautiful spot. You could see back for miles, right back in fact across the island studded broadwater to Surfers' with the tops of its high-rise buildings gilded pink and gold in the setting sun and against a backdrop of dark, boiling clouds heralding a storm coming in from the sea.

But this beach and park was far removed, not only by miles but in spirit, from Surfers' Paradise. The protected broadwater lapped the sand gently and a group of kids were playing with a dog, their bikes piled in a tangled heap on the grass. There was a lone fisherman sitting on a collapsible canvas stool and wearing a disreputable but obviously cherished hat.

Then a piercing hooroo came from one of the houses on the other side of the road and the kids abandoned their game reluctantly, had a cheerful fight for their bikes and all raced home, leaving only the fisherman.

And Giles and India.

'I,' she paused a little painfully. ' . . . It was different for me. But it's very hard to explain why without ... without ...' She stopped and shrugged.

'Without calling your feelings for my father into doubt? I'm not trying to make you do that, India,' Giles said quietly.

She stared out of the window and felt a playful breeze lift her hair.

'Perhaps I ought to start at the beginning then,' she said finally. 'When I first met your ... Rod, although I was nearly twenty, I was horribly shy and I could count the number of dates I'd been out on, on one hand. They'd all been disasters anyway. My mother used to tease me sometimes and tell me I was a very late developer—perhaps I was. Later, though,' she said drily, 'than even she thought.' She turned her head and their gaze caught and held and she saw that he knew what she meant, and coloured faintly.

'Go on,' he murmured.

'But with Rod it was different, I loved him in a way before I ever thought of ... sleeping with him. He made me feel safe and secure, and *happy*. And for the first time in my life, not *painfully* shy, although I still was for a long time.'

'Shy of him making love to you?'

'Yes,' she whispered, and blinked away a tear. 'But I needn't have been—I don't know why I was. He was so gentle and sweet and ... well, I progressed to the stage where I began to enjoy it and I could relax about it and even start to ... give a little in return. That made it—I don't know, very special. It gave him so much pleasure. But it was so *little*,' she said with sudden intensity.

'Do you mean it wasn't enough for you?'

'No, I don't mean that,' she said angrily. 'It was

more than enough for me. I was perfectly content, and happy beyond belief. Only, you can't live in a plastic bubble, can you? And there seemed to be always someone, if not saying something snide, looking it. I could always detect those "My, my what a young wife he's got himself," looks. Or the "I wonder if he'll last the distance" kind of looks. Not to mention,' she said bitterly, 'the kind that said, "I could show you a lot your old man couldn't". Lance Kidder specialised in those.'

'I'm sorry,' Giles said. 'I . . .'

'Oh, it was different in a way with you,' India cut in wearily. 'You never—I mean, you hated me whole-heartedly. The one thing you never did was show any desire to . . . show me a thing or two yourself.'

He moved abruptly, but she went on without looking at him, 'In a curious way, I respected you for that. I suppose it's possible to respect an . . . adversary. But that's beside the point.'

'Tell me the point.'

'The point is that I was a perfectly satisfied, happy wife, yet no one seemed to be able to believe it. And now,' she concluded shakily, 'I'm beginning to understand why. You made me see how . . . passive I'd really been with Rod. You turned sex for me into something quite different, something electric and devastating where I seemed to have no control, no will, no . . .'

'India,' Giles said a little grimly, 'I don't know why it torments you so.'

'Then I'll tell you! What if it had happened when Rod was alive? What if I'd discovered then that some man could make me mindless with desire, especially some man who hated me, and vice versa? Do you know, Giles, I really wish you'd left me the way I was. It made your father very happy . . .'

'Of course it did,' he agreed harshly. 'And don't think he didn't go out of his way to preserve the status quo!'

'What do you mean?' she whispered at last, her eyes wide and wary.

'I'm surprised you noticed as much of the reactions to your marriage as you did, India,' he said curtly, 'because he kept you virtually locked up in an ivory tower.'

'He didn't!'

'Oh yes, he did.'

'I . . , it wasn't anything I didn't want,' she said, and bit her lip.

'I'm not saying that. What I'm trying to explain to you is that he . . . shielded you from a whole lot of things. For his own very personal reasons.'

'Because *he* knew how cynical people could be. Why shouldn't he have done that?' she countered.

'It was more than that,' Giles returned flatly. 'You say you now realise how—passive you were, but he wouldn't have wanted you to be any other way. *I* saw it. You basically knew it, subconsciously. Why do you think he hated you dancing with anyone else, for instance?'

She stared at him. 'I don't know what you're trying to say.'

'The thing he loved most about you, India, was your innocence, that childlike trust and devotion. It enchanted him and meant . . . everything to him. It was what he wanted to protect at all costs. And I don't blame him,' he added. 'That kind of innocence and purity is like a rare flower you don't often find these days.'

It was a long time before she spoke and then it was in a voice that shook. 'Where does that leave me now? And how do you know all this?'

'Then you accept it?' He reached across and made her look at him with his fingers beneath her chin.

'I . . . are you trying to say it was a . . . father and daughter kind of relationship?' she whispered.

'In a sense. There's nothing wrong in it, India. It happens often. He *wasn't* your father but he represented . . . wisdom, security, some of the things you lacked. Many young girls marry for that and are very happy, like you were.'

'Would . . . would I always have been happy?' Her involuntary words seemed to echo. 'Would he?' she added, as if she'd burnt her boats behind her.

'That's academic now,' Giles said. 'It's also foolish to torture yourself wondering about it. But for what it's worth, I think towards the end he realised that you had to grow and mature, that he couldn't keep you solely for himself always. That's why he brought you into the business and . . . opened up your life a little. He must have loved you very much to have put that ahead of how he really wanted to keep you, like a bud, unfurling but never to blossom.'

She repeated, with her eyes closed and tears on her cheeks, 'How do you know all this?'

He shrugged. 'Intuition, and the fact that I knew him quite well. He was, in some ways, a disillusioned cynic himself. He'd seen it all—a failed marriage that turned into a vicious nightmare. Many women over the years—I don't mean he was particularly promiscuous, but he had the opportunity to remarry time and time and again. He took none of them. So it wasn't especially difficult to work out that there was something very different about you. Unfortunately, although I worked it out, I let several factors cloud my judgment as to what it actually was. I ... decided,' he hesitated, 'that he was trying to relive his youth, and of course that you, with an eye to the main chance, were only too happy to help him,' he said drily.

India opened her eyes at last and realised that it was raining, that the storm had caught up with them and it was almost dark. 'Thank you,' she said huskily.

He smiled without humour. 'What for?'

'For ... understanding in the end. For helping me to understand.'

'I wonder if I have.'

She looked at him questioningly.

'There is still the matter of us, India,' he said a little grimly. 'Do you understand about that too?'

She trembled. 'Not entirely.'

'I thought not,' he said sardonically, and she shivered at the way his hands gripped the wheel briefly.

'Giles ...'

'No,' he cut in and turned abruptly to pull her into his arms. 'Before you say anything else,' he continued, his lips barely moving and his eyes roaming her startled, pale face, 'let me put it this way ... will you marry me, India?'

She gasped and his eyes glittered with sudden mockery. 'What did you think I had in mind for us?'

She was unable to speak and she realised that her heart was pounding like a train.

'Did you think I was looking for a mistress, or someone to share a few nights with? Is that what you thought, India? Tell me, I'm interested.' His voice was hard and challenging. 'I must have come across rather brutally,' he added.

She found her voice. 'You didn't . . .you, no you *didn't*, but . .'

'But what? The old story—we don't know each other very well?' he queried with ruthless intensity. 'Surely that's wearing a bit thin by now? After all, we've known each other for five years . . . one way or another,' he said in a suddenly low, husky voice. 'There's a great deal I know about you, anyway. For example . . .'

'Don't,' she whispered.

'I wasn't going to—not yet. I was going to say that I know you're always beautiful, sometimes surprisingly timid about some things, which fascinates me, yet extraordinarily brave about others. I've seen you walk into board meetings with your head held high, knowing full well I was going to throw you to the lions, in a manner of speaking. I know that you could have cut the last tie between me and my father any time you wanted to, but you didn't. Oh, it got cut, but not by you.' He stopped, and when he spoke again his voice was quite different. 'And of course I know all the things you don't want me to mention. Why don't you? You were the perfect lover . . .'

She swallowed and heard the rain hammering on the roof of the car, in unison it seemed with a sort of hammering uncertainty within her mind.

'What is it you want to know about me then?'

he said after a long, agonising silence during which she'd tried unsuccessfully to speak. 'I've more or less told you my life story. What more do you want to know?'

'That we ... *love* each other,' she said then, goaded at last into speech.

'You mean you still can't believe that it could happen? Or that for some reason we still haven't exorcised, you're determined not to let it happen? Why don't you just admit you're fighting against thunder, India? Look, I'll show you ...'

'Giles, no,' she begged, 'I can't think ...'

'There's nothing to think about.' He spoke into her hair. 'This is the answer, don't you see?' He kissed her temples, her eyelids, her throat and then her lips and she couldn't for the life of her resist him. Perhaps he's right, she thought. What else could it be ...?

He said at last, when his mouth left hers, 'Will you come home with me?'

She could only nod against his shoulder.

Home, she was surprised to find, was a house on the water at Runaway Bay.

The garage door was radio-controlled from the car and it slid noiselessly down behind them. There was a door into the house from the garage. India hesitated briefly before stepping through it.

He took her hand.

'I didn't know ... I assumed you lived in Surfers'.'

'I used to, but with a boat this is much handier. I have my own jetty.' He led her into the lounge, switching on a couple of lamps and one wall switch, and took her over to the wide windows with billowing curtains, and pulled them open so that she could see out.

It was an outside light he'd switched on, and it illuminated a green stretch of damp lawn and the jetty with a sleek cabin cruiser tied up to it.

He let the curtain drop and said, 'Hungry now?'

India smiled ruefully. 'A bit. Can I . . .?'

'No, I'm fairly domesticated. Well, enough to rustle up a snack.' He smiled wryly. 'Have a look around if you'd like to,' he added.

The lounge was comfortably furnished with a brown velvet suite, a magnificent Bokhara rug with a tree of life formation laid over the champagne coloured wall-to-wall carpet, and matt cream hessian papered walls. The large round coffee table had a beaten copper top and on it was a brilliant green malachite box that looked very old. The lampshades were all of gold foil, so the lighting was soft but radiant.

India wandered down the thickly carpeted passage looking briefly into three bedrooms, a study with an overflowing desk, a television and a modern, very comfortable-looking leather recliner chair. She found a luxurious, midnight blue tiled bathroom and washed her hands and stared at herself in the mirror.

There were faint shadows beneath her eyes, witness to several sleepless nights. But the curious thing was, it was like looking at another person, someone she didn't really know . . .

She hesitated outside one room that lay in darkness next to the lounge, guessing it must be a dining room. Then she shrugged and felt for a light switch—and immediately wondered if she'd been possessed by ESP. Because the first thing she saw on the opposite wall was her painting, the one of the empty Abbot's chair.

She stared at it and wondered why she'd ever allowed herself to be persuaded to put it up for sale, because she'd hoped that by transmitting her intense loneliness and grief to canvas she could ease the pain. But of course it had been there to stare back at her, so she'd let it go. And, she thought with a sudden pang, that's what precipitated . . . this. How strange.

She didn't hear Giles come up behind her, so absorbed was she; she only felt him sliding his arms around her waist. She leaned back against him after a moment of tension. But wasn't that the strangest thing of all? she reflected. How her body always surrendered for her, to him?

'India,' he said after a time, and turned her round to face him, 'it's over now, isn't it? You don't ever have to feel lonely again.'

She stared up, deep into his grey eyes and a shudder went through her body as she laid her cheek against his chest. 'No,' she whispered.

'Are you going to marry me?'

'Yes.'

'When?' He was holding her very close.

'Whenever you like.'

'That might be sooner than you think,' he said wryly. 'I . . .' But he stopped as if he'd changed his mind. 'As soon as it can be arranged?'

'If you want to,' she murmured, and moved to pull away but only so that she could free her arms and wind them round his neck with a queer little sound in her throat.

*　　*　　*

He said later, much later, 'My sandwiches will be ruined.'

'What kind were they?'

'Chicken and tomato.'

'Have you got any eggs?'

'I . . . yes, I guess so. Why?'

'You could scrap off the chicken and tomato and make an omelette with it.'

'I could try, but I've never made a successful omelette in my life.'

She laughed softly and stretched luxuriously. 'I thought you said you were very domesticated?'

'Oh, I am. I make great sandwiches . . . Was it any good for you?' he added abruptly, half sitting up and leaning over to look into her eyes.

She considered the matter with her lips twitching slightly, and looked around. The main bedroom of the house at Runaway Bay was rather austerely masculine—the same champagne wall-to-wall carpet, sage green curtains and bedspread and a brass handled, cedar chest of drawers. But there was nothing austere about the way she was lying naked beside him in a pool of golden light from the bedside lamp. Nor had there been much austerity about their love-making. He'd kissed every part of her body from her toes to her hair, but refusing to allow her to do anything at all but submit to his wandering lips until she'd been quivering with desire, moaning low and sweet in her throat with it and writhing against the sheet with the intensity of it. 'It was,' she said with a sudden catch in her voice, '. . . I can't tell you. Don't you know?'

'I know . . . that it frightens you sometimes,' he said with an effort. He touched her mouth then slid his fingers down towards her breasts. 'And that afterwards is when the doubts come crowding in. I'd like to think we've banished all those now?' He looked at her searchingly.

'I . . .' She stopped. Had that been a camera-like sensation in her mind again? A high-speed shutter clicking? No, she decided. I've finished with that. 'Yes,' she said tremulously, 'we have.' She kissed the smooth skin of his shoulder with an open mouth. 'I want you. I need you,' she murmured. 'I love you.'

'India,' he tugged gently at her hair until she looked up at him, 'do you really mean that?'

Her lips quivered mischievously. 'How can I not mean it? You have me here at your mercy—unfed and with only the prospect of stale chicken and tomato sandwiches before me . . .'

'I had a bottle of champagne too.'

She laughed, then sobered suddenly. 'Giles, why do you live in this house? On your own?'

'I don't see how that follows.'

'Tell me.'

'I—it was a whim, really.'

'Not because of your boat?' She kissed and stroked his upper arm.

'Not entirely,' he said slowly, and slid his fingers through her hair. 'I'd never lived in a house before—at least not that I could remember. Units, apartments, hotels . . . what's wrong?' he asked, as she laid her cheek against his arm with a little sigh.

'Nothing. I haven't either. Not one that could be called home. Not one where you could dig in the garden.'

'You can do that here,' he said softly.

CHAPTER EIGHT

INDIA hummed a little tune to keep her spirits up as she sorted through a cupboard. Two days ago she'd agreed to marry Giles Ballantyne, yesterday he'd had to leave for Sydney for two days at the most, he'd said, and she was back at her unit, preparing to leave it in a matter of a week or so, after five years of living there.

She'd reached the bottom shelf and she sat back on her heels and sighed suddenly. What to take and what to leave to be sold? she wondered. Perhaps I'm best off just taking myself only . . . so much here is like a part of me. I should have gone with him, he wanted me to. Maybe I should never have come back . . .?

It had been business that had taken Giles to Sydney, and India had come sufficiently out of her rather dazed frame of mind to think suddenly about all the things she'd forgotten since leaving Hamilton Island. Like the island she'd never got to see that Ballantyne's was going to develop, and the take-over bid Lance Kidder had mentioned.

She'd asked Giles if this trip was anything to do with the take-over bid, and by way of reply he'd kissed her, and murmured yes—but not to worry, he had it all under control. She'd been only too happy to leave it at that but when he'd suggested her going to Sydney with him, she'd thought of herself sitting around in hotels, waiting for him, and had decided not to. He'd hesitated for a moment, then not pressed her.

But when she'd driven him to Coolangatta Airport, he'd held her very close in the departure lounge and then said as he'd said once before with a funny little smile, 'Don't go away, will you?'

'As if I could,' she'd replied huskily.

The doorbell rang, breaking into her reverie, and her heart started to hammer in case it was Giles. But it was Lance Kidder, of all people, standing on the doorstep.

'Hello, India,' he said quietly. 'May I come in?'

She stared at him until he smiled ruefully. 'It's business, actually,' he murmured.

'I . . . oh,' she said a little helplessly, 'all right.'

He followed her into the lounge and looked around admiringly. 'Perfect,' he said finally, 'a perfect setting for you. Rod was a very lucky man, and a very discerning one.'

India turned away abruptly, then she recovered herself and took refuge in politeness. 'Can I get you a drink or coffee?'

'No, thank you. I,' he paused and looked at her keenly, 'I was wondering whether congratulations mightn't be the order of the day?'

'I don't know what you mean,' India replied.

Lance Kidder smiled indulgently, his dark eyes still curiously probing. 'I was quite sure Giles would have popped the question by now,' he said.

India went stiff with shock. 'How did . . .?' She stopped and bit her lip.

'How did I know?' Kidder offered, and she coloured faintly.

'Yes.' There seemed to be no point in dissembling.

'Well, I'll tell you,' Lance Kidder said very seriously, and with no trace of any of his former contempt of manner. 'May I sit down?' He took her consent for granted and after a moment she sat down in the Abbot's chair. 'It first dawned on me what he had in mind when he took you to Hamilton Island, India.'

'I don't see how it could have . . .'

'It *was* a . . . complete reversal of his normal . . . er . . . treatment of you, wasn't it?' he asked.

India flushed. 'Lance,' she said, but he held up a hand and cut in quietly.

'Please let me finish. To me at least it was a significant enough change for me to—wonder. However, that's all I did until after you'd been gone for a couple of days. Then in my position of deputising for Giles while he was away, I came into the possession of some rather startling information.' He shot her a keen glance but she could only look back at him bewilderedly. 'To do with this take-over bid,' he said.

'I don't understand.'

'I thought you might not have. Has Giles told you anything about it? By the way, he was very . . . angry at the way you left Hamilton Island so abruptly.'

'I . . . it was a misunderstanding,' she said awkwardly.

'So I gathered. One that's been rectified, though?'

India moved uncomfortably. 'Lance, I don't know what your point is . . .'

'It's this,' he cut in. 'Before he left for Hamilton, Giles was the only one of us who realised what a serious take-over bid this was. But if I've done my homework correctly now and assessed the shares that have already changed hands, plus what still *could* change hands—and believe me, India, I owe no allegiance to Giles Ballantyne and he knows it—if I've worked it all out correctly, by a stroke of fate *you* could again be in the position of having the casting vote, so to speak.'

India stared at him with her lips parted.

'Do you understand what I mean? Your shares form the balance of power. If you sold out, Ballantyne's would be swallowed up into a much larger organisation. A thing Giles would hate, no doubt, although for my part, I think it would be a good thing.'

India's hands started to tremble and she clutched them in her lap. 'I . . .'

Lance Kidder waited, then when she couldn't organise her thoughts into words, he said, 'By some form of blackmail or another, Giles has manipulated you for a long time now, India. But he couldn't hope to do it always, could he? I mean, once you'd got over Rod,' he said delicately, 'it was very much on the cards that you'd meet someone and fall in love—again,' he added with the barest hesitation and a swift downward glance. 'And even discounting that possibility, his . . . power over you had to wane finally, hadn't it?' He stared at her, challenging her to deny this.

'What . . . what are you *saying*, Lance?' she asked at last.

He smiled almost gently. 'I think you know what I'm saying, India,' he replied, 'but I'll put it more simply. Giles has found himself in a position with his back to the wall. A position where *you* hold the future of Ballantyne's in the palm of your hand. And he decided to secure that future in the one sure way, in the same way he accused us of . . . desiring to secure our futures at the last board meeting. Only he's going a step further. He's going to marry you to do it.'

India closed her eyes and went white. 'I only have your word for that, Lance,' she said tightly, and her lashes flew up. 'The word of a man who hates Giles for reasons of ambition, the word of a man who can see a better future for himself this way.'

Lance Kidder shrugged. 'I won't waste my time denying it,' he responded, and there was a flash of sudden anger in his eyes. 'But as for doubting my word, why don't you check up with Jeff Whitby? You trust his word, don't you? But if you still find yourself doubting, India, why don't you simply ask yourself just what else would account for the fact that Giles went from despising you and hating you—and never losing an opportunity to let the world know about it—to wanting to marry you, all in the matter of a few days.'

'Get out, Lance,' she whispered fiercely. 'If you only knew how I despised *you*!'

He shrugged and stood up. 'Think about it,' he said. 'And while you're doing that why don't you consider selling out to the opposition, India? And freeing yourself, once and, for all, from this . . . mess.'

CHAPTER NINE

'WELL, Mrs Ballantyne, not far to go now.'

India swam up through clouds of drowsiness. She'd never felt so tired in her life. 'Giles?' she whispered, then bit her lip and wiped the sweat off her forehead with the back of her hand. 'How long?' she asked hoarsely, and gripped a comforting hand that was slipped into hers.

'If you just do as we tell you, pet, it will all be over in a few minutes,' another voice said. 'You've been great. Now ...'

Oh God, oh God ... help me, India thought dimly. Then she could no longer think, could only go along with the forces of her body ...

'Well, we have a ... boy.' The clinical voice of the lady doctor was not quite so clinical all of a sudden. 'A redhead too, and as babies go, a beauty by the look of him. There, there,' she said as India burst into tears, 'see for yourself ...'

India stared out through the french windows of her room as the sun set. It was an autumnal May evening and her son lay fast asleep in his crib beside the bed. The best-looking baby on the whole floor, the sister assured her, but India guessed she told all new Mums that. But there was no doubt that baby Ballantyne generated some interest. Perhaps on account of the definitely gingery down on his head, or his plump, beautiful little cheeks or his perfectly formed, quite long body. 'Going to be tall, you are, my prince,' the nurse, who came to help India bathe him, said. 'A real heart-breaker, I reckon, like your . . .' She'd clamped her lips shut suddenly and looked intensely annoyed with herself.

But India had given no indication that she'd known only too well what the nurse had been going to say. *Like your father* . . . And the nurse had relaxed but she hadn't known that India was quite well aware that there was a certain buzz of speculation surrounding her and her baby. She'd accidentally overheard the sister saying to someone, 'It's just not fair, not a soul to come and see her and the baby—I'd like to get my hands on whoever the father is! Bet he has red hair too . . .'

'You mustn't blame him, he doesn't know,' India had whispered, but to herself, and had looked at her baby with suddenly tormented, questioning eyes.

But that was undoubtedly another reason why Baby Ballantyne generated a lot of interest—his seeming lack of any relations, but especially a father. India couldn't help but feel tearfully grateful to the kindly women nursing on the Maternity floor, who tried in small ways to make up for this, so that her room was never lonely for long. Outside the quiet confines of the hospital, teemed the cosmopolitan life of the city of Sydney. Which she had to go back to shortly, India reminded herself that chilly evening, with a sigh.

'Why the sigh?' the doctor queried, coming quietly into the room. 'Anything wrong?'

'No,' India denied hastily. 'No, I'm fine.'

The doctor who was in her late thirties, India

judged, and projected a calm, capable image and often looked weary, shot her a probing glance and sat down on the bed suddenly. 'Mrs Ballantyne,' she said, 'we've known each other for some months now haven't we?'

'Yes,' India agreed cautiously, after a moment.

'During which time I have refrained from asking you any personal questions, have I not? Because that seemed to be the way you wanted it?'

'I . . . do.'

'My dear,' that calm, tired face softened a little, 'I don't want to know any particulars, but I do want to make sure that *you* are very sure in your mind that you're going about this in the right way. Was he a married man?'

India stared at her. 'No,' she said at last, 'in fact he wanted to marry me. But for all the wrong reasons, I think. Unfortunately, when I worked it out and . . . left him, I hadn't taken into consideration that I might be pregnant.'

'These wrong reasons,' the doctor said quietly, 'what were they?'

India twisted her head restlessly against the pillows. 'It's like a . . . fairy story,' she said finally. 'I would never have imagined it could happen to me.'

'They say fact is often stranger than fiction,' the doctor commented wryly. 'Look here, you're my last patient this evening. If you'd like to tell me all about it, I have the time and the willingness to listen. But it's up to you.'

'I . . .' India hesitated, then the words started to pour forth, like a spring that had been stopped up too long . . .

'So you're quite convinced he wanted to marry

you to get control of your shares?' the doctor asked at last.

'When I found out what the situation was,' India said very quietly, 'I suddenly knew that there'd been something wrong all the time—that I'd known at the back of my mind, but I'd never been able to pin it down. It's hard to explain,' she wiped her eyes, 'but there was always *something* that didn't quite . . . jell.'

'So you just upped and left?'

India laid her head back. 'More or less. Oh, don't think I wanted to believe it! By then, you see, I was hopelessly in love. But,' she sniffed, 'it accounted for so many things apart from that feeling I'd had. The suddenness of it all, the . . . urgency about getting married, the last thing he ever said to me, as if he was afraid of what I might do if I found out. The fact that he never *told* me how serious the take-over thing was. And you see, I knew how much . . . his father's firm meant to him.'

'What did you do?'

'I . . . there was one ally I had on the board. I contacted him and he verified it all. So I took him into my confidence, in a way. I told him that I wanted out, that it was what I should have done long before, that I wanted Giles to have my shares but that it was impossible for me to deal direct with him. I . . . managed to convince him with some difficulty, and we worked out a solution. I knew he was a hundred per cent loyal to Giles, so I sold *him* my shares, through a broker of course, on the understanding that he would re-sell them to Giles. I resigned from the board. It seemed to be the only way to . . . escape.'

'And you disappeared?'

'That was a lot easier to do. Giles was—I told you that he was away at the time. Well, he was delayed another two days.'

'Have you ever heard what happened?'

'No. Deliberately,' India said bleakly. 'I didn't want to know.'

'I see,' the doctor said slowly. 'You know, I think you did one thing wrong. You've told me you loved the man but you never gave him a chance to defend himself.'

'For a very good reason,' India whispered. 'I had a tendency to keel over like a pack of cards for him. To lose all my judgment, everything. And I decided that the time had come for me to trust my own instinct, that voice that had tried to tell me all along that something just didn't fit. You see, I can't really blame him—his own father had been the one who caused it all, with me as an accomplice.'

'But an unwitting one, my dear.'

India agreed wearily. 'All the same, I knew I couldn't bear to hear the truth from him.'

'Very well,' the doctor conceded at last. 'But there's another factor in the game now, isn't there? His child. Do you think you're being fair to *either* of them?'

India closed her eyes. 'If you only knew,' she said huskily. 'That's the awful irony of it all.' She reached out to touch the crib. 'This is exactly how I came into the world, with no father. You'd think I'd be the last person to do that to any child of mine, wouldn't you? But it's only now that it's happened to me, that I really understand my mother's dilemma.'

'She never told your father?'

'No. He never knew I existed. And it was only when she died that I discovered, when I was going through her papers, that he'd died a couple of years previously. She'd written to him, just as a long-lost friend I gathered, and received a note from his wife with the news. I've always wondered if she'd decided, at long last, to tell him about me—and left it too late.'

'For what it's worth, if you're prepared to take some unbiased advice, Mrs Ballantyne,' the doctor said, 'don't do that to yourself and this child. At least let his father know! It may not solve anything, it may make it harder for you, but I believe he has a right to know. And I believe the child has a right. How did you feel about your father?'

It was a long time before India answered. 'I feel now that I'd give almost anything to have known him, that it's as if there's a part of myself that I can never know. When I was a child I was too afraid to think too much about him because my mother had explained that I could ... complicate his life terribly. I was sure he would have to hate me.'

'Then don't you think it's your duty to your son to allow him, and his father, to make their own judgments? And if nothing else, provide your child with the other half of his identity?'

Winter in Brisbane, India thought irrelevantly, is not that cold. Not nearly as cold as the state of my heart, she mused. Cold with panic ... In fact she wasn't in Brisbane but on the coast, close by. She'd flown up from Sydney and taken a room in a motel with a garden. Richard was now three months old, and he'd slept serenely through the flight and had accepted their new circumstances with equanimity.

They'd only been on the coast for a day, however, and India had told herself that she'd wait to see how he settled down until she did anything. A similar thing to what she'd told herself when she'd left hospital with him, with the doctor's advice still ringing in her ears and branded into her brain. For two reasons—the almost overflowing love for this baby who had taken her heart by storm, and a correspondingly genuine desire to see his first few months of life free of trauma; and because she didn't really have the courage to face Giles and confront him with his son.

But Richard had thrived on her plentiful supply of milk, and there came a day when she had to admit that he was a happy, healthy, contented baby, and the longer she put it off, the harder it was going to be. After all, she had come to believe, however belatedly, that she'd been wrong to decide to keep this baby to herself and for herself. To let history repeat itself and let another child have to suffer the consequences—although he still might do that. But at least he would know. And Giles was one person, who, apart from anything else, knew how vulnerable children are, she had told herself. Surely he would understand that they could come to some sort of arrangement where Richard could know both his parents . . .

She sat on the motel bed and stared at the phone for a long time, then she took a deep breath and asked for a number.

'Connecting you,' the receptionist said, and

another disembodied voice spoke into her ear. 'Paradise Resorts. Can I help you?'

'I . . . I beg your pardon,' India stammered.

'Paradise Resorts incorporating Ballantyne Enterprises,' the voice said patiently. 'Can I help you?'

'I . . . could I speak to Mr Ballantyne, please? Mr Giles Ballantyne?'

There was a slight hesitation. Then the girl at the other end said, 'I'm afraid Mr Ballantyne is no longer connected with this organisation. If your call is of a business nature, I could connect you to Mr Kidder, our Managing Director.'

India's mouth dropped open and she went white and removed the phone from her ear and stared at it for a moment. When she put it back the girl was saying, 'Hello! Are you there?'

'Yes,' India said, and swallowed. 'Um . . . no . . . oh! Would it be possible to speak to Mrs Fiona Hardcastle? I'm sorry to be a nuisance, but I . . . I used to work for Ballantyne's,' she said lamely.

'Mrs Hardcastle has retired. However, I do have a forwarding address, I think . . . yes. Have you got a pen?'

India reached for her bag hastily, and a few moments later put the phone down and stared before her with horrified eyes. 'What went wrong?' she whispered.

'What went wrong, Fiona?'

'Oh, my dear Mrs Ballantyne,' Fiona said with a break in her voice.

'Please call me India—you always used to when we first knew each other,' India begged.

'Sit down then, love,' Fiona advised. 'You look

as if you've seen a ghost. You were lucky to catch me in! I've become a great bowler in my retirement. Would you like a cup of tea? I think you could do with one.'

India swallowed. 'I'd love one,' she said honestly, 'and I'm sorry to have burst in on you like this, I'm staying at a motel not far from here. But I don't want to make you late . . .'

'If you think I'd dream of going to bowls now,' Fiona said contemptuously, 'you don't know me very well. I've wondered and worried about you, India, almost as if you were my own daughter!'

'I'm sorry,' India whispered, and did battle with some weak tears—a battle she lost.

But twenty minutes later or so she was seated at Fiona's kitchen table, she was calm again and sipping her tea gratefully.

'What went wrong?' Fiona enquired reflectively. 'I don't honestly know. If anyone had told me that Giles Ballantyne would sell out his father's company to the opposition, I'd have laughed at them! But that's just what he did.'

'Did he have to, though? I mean, did he lose the controlling interest? Don't tell me Jeff let me down?' she asked fearfully.

'No, he didn't. I was taking notes at the board meeting when it all happened. Mr Whitby . . . tendered your letter of resignation and let it be known that your shares were now in his possession, with an option to purchase only open to Mr Ballantyne. Otherwise they would stay in his possession, he said, and would be used to block any take-over bid of the company. It was an extremely dramatic board meeting, India, and I've seen a few.

'Mr Ballantyne had only got home from Sydney that morning and he arrived at the office looking demented. Nothing to how Mr Kidder looked, however, when Mr Whitby had had his say. He was absolutely furious. He said some incredible things to Giles, and some unpleasant things about you. Which,' Fiona said slowly, 'shed some light for me on what must have happened, India. Oh, I never liked Lance Kidder, so it was easy to see through the venom and the malice.'

'Go on,' India insisted.

'Well, then Mr Ballantyne turned on him and for a moment or two I quite thought he was going to murder Kidder. He said "You told her I was marrying her to get control of her shares?" And Kidder replied, "Oh, come on, Giles! We're all adults. Of course you were! Let's face it. What I can't understand is why you didn't do it long ago—I'm not blaming you for it," he said. "She's a mighty marriageable woman. Only you didn't see it, did you, Giles? I must say that's what stuck in my throat. You were so damned superior because you'd never lusted after her. But did I laugh at the thought of you taking her up to Hamilton Island to woo her—I mean, it was really ironic wasn't it?"'

Fiona broke off and sighed. 'I remember it all so well, as if it was yesterday. And when Kidder said that, that's when I really thought Mr Ballantyne would kill him. So did Mr Whitby. But for once in his life George Ramsey did something useful—he complained about pains in his chest. That more or less brought Mr Ballantyne back to his senses. He got up and walked out.'

'What happened then?' India asked with her heart in her mouth.

'Two days later, Mr Ballantyne called another board meeting, but this time he was the one with the startling news. And it only lasted for about five minutes. He announced that he'd purchased your shares from Mr Whitby and sold them at the same price, together with his own, to Paradise Resorts. He said that he'd been offered the Managing Directorship of the new company, that he'd refused it, but had negotiated positions for all those employed by Ballantyne's if they were interested. He thanked Mr Whitby for his support and me,' Fiona looked a little misty-eyed, 'for my loyalty to him and his father. That was all. The only other time I saw him was later that day. He called me into his office and discussed the new company with me briefly and asked me if I would be staying on. I said no, that I was thinking of retiring anyway. Then he asked me if I had any idea where you might be. I racked my brains, but I couldn't come up with anything.' She looked at India reproachfully.

'I'm sorry,' India said shakily. 'I just felt I had to go.'

'Well,' Fiona mused, 'I mightn't have been able to keep a secret, who knows? But I do know he went to great lengths to track you down. I overheard him talking to Jeff Whitby that same afternoon. He said he'd managed to get from a real estate agent that you'd put the unit on the market, giving them sole agency, and that they were to deal with a solicitor who had your power of attorney, but that the solicitor had maintained that they were not at liberty to reveal your whereabouts and anyway, they didn't know it.'

'What did Jeff say?'

'He . . . seemed to be apologising up to a point. But he did say something abut not being in the possession of the full facts, and anyway he'd felt honour bound to respect your wishes. Actually, he and I were the only two who left, apart from Mr Ballantyne. But I did stay on for a few months to help the transition go smoothly.'

India stared at her. 'But *why* did he do it?' she asked painfully.

Fiona stared thoughtfully back. 'I told you,' she said at length, 'I don't know. India,' her eyes narrowed, 'there's something different about you. What is it?'

India turned away abruptly.

'Tell me, love,' Fiona said gently. 'You used to confide in me.'

'I . . . I've got a baby,' India whispered.

Fiona's mouth dropped open. 'You mean . . .?' she said finally.

'Yes. Giles's.'

'And he doesn't know?' Fiona looked aghast.

'No. *I* didn't know I was pregnant when I left. Then I . . .' She tailed off.

'You found you weren't coping too well?'

India bit her lip. 'It wasn't that, really. Thanks to . . . this baby's grandfather,' she said, and winced, 'I'm pretty well off.'

'But you came to tell Giles all the same?'

India stood up abruptly. 'Yes. But now . . . things have changed.'

Fiona thought for a bit. 'Where is it?' she said at last.

'I left him at the motel with a babysitter. I should be getting back . . .'

Fiona stared at her, still obviously somewhat bemused, then a look of her old, brisk decisiveness crossed her face and she stood up too. 'We'll go and get him. No!' she held up a hand, 'don't you say a word. You're coming to stay with me. I've got plenty of room, a pretty garden, fresh sea air, and since Tom died I rattle round here like a ghost. Besides, you're looking a bit thin, India, and pale. If you're feeding this baby you need to keep your strength up. Now don't argue with me!'

India went to sleep that night with an odd feeling of warmth in her heart.

It was impossible not to be grateful to Fiona and touched by her. She'd fallen in love with Richard on sight, and for the first time since India had left hospital, there had been someone on hand to help bath him, to admire him, to talk to . . .

There was also, as India discovered the next day, a sense of home about Fiona's house that she hadn't realised she'd missed—or failed to create in Sydney.

It was beautifully situated on Currumbin Hill, with a magnificent view over the ocean north towards Surfers' and the mouth of Currumbin Creek, and while it wasn't large, and was quite old, it had that air of being lived in. And the garden was a dream—Fiona's husband had loved gardening apparently, and by some miracle had created an English garden in this seaside, sub-tropical spot.

'Being up high helps a bit,' Fiona said as India admired it the next morning. 'The air is not so salty nor the soil so sandy, but I still have to nourish it a lot. And without these windbreaks Tom grew, it wouldn't be possible,' she added, waving towards a high leafy hedge and a thicket of bamboo.

India stared at the riot of climbing roses, the sweet peas just coming into bloom, the primulas and budding marigolds, and felt a shaft of pain pierce her heart. Had she given up a garden to dig in for all the wrong reasons? she wondered.

'Now,' Fiona said over an enormous lunch that day, when Richard was asleep in his collapsible pram on the patio, 'what are you going to do?'

'I don't know,' India replied after a time. 'I feel like an actor without a script. If only I could work out why Giles did it!'

'Personally, I don't see that it makes much difference,' Fiona looked at India steadily. 'Tell me what difference it makes?'

India closed her eyes. 'I don't *know*,' she said intensely. 'But ... I'm more afraid than ever, somehow. You don't know what Giles can be like. None of you,' she added as Fiona moved, 'really know what he was like to me before ...'

'Well, I guessed,' Fiona conceded, and frowned. 'After his father died he wasn't particularly discreet about it. I often wondered ...' She stopped with a sigh. 'I don't know, I really don't know! But it's still his baby, India.'

'I know, but honestly, Fiona, it doesn't add up, does it?'

'Well,' Fiona hesitated and then seemed to change her mind, 'perhaps the best thing to do is let him explain for himself.'

'What's he doing now?'

'I don't know,' Fiona admitted helplessly. 'I asked him that last day he was there and he said he hadn't made up his mind. But he was very good to me, you know, India. He made me promise that if ever I needed anything I wouldn't hesitate to let him know. He knew that Tom had died, of course, and that we'd never had children. And he said to me, "I've often felt that you've made Ballantyne's your family, Mrs Hardcastle. I'd like to repay that." I know he meant that if ever I was ill and alone and so on, he'd like to help out.'

'I think I need a few days to try and think things out,' India said tremulously.

Fiona eyed her shrewdly then she nodded after a moment. 'It won't do any harm. And in the meantime, I can fatten you up and make an old fool of myself over Master Richard. Do you know, I think he smiled at me this morning!'

'I'm sure he did,' India said warmly. 'He's really getting the hang of it now, smiling.'

The days slipped by until nearly a week had passed. One part of India was more relaxed than she'd been for a long time, she realised, relaxed and responsive to care and attention and companionship. I never understood how much you need that, she thought. How having a baby on your own is about the loneliest thing you can do, however much you love it.

But there was still that unanswered question hanging over her, that decision to be made; that awful, nameless fear in her heart that didn't seem to be quite the same fear as the other one, the old fear of confronting Giles with his baby and seeing him revert to his old, mercilessly contemptuous treatment of her.

Or is it all the same thing? she asked herself torturedly one afternoon. I wish I knew ... The other thing is, I can't impose on Fiona for ever, much as I'd like to, and I see as every day goes past, that questioning look growing in her eyes. Not, I know, because she wants to be rid of me, but because, like the doctor, she thinks there is only one thing for me to do.

Today, she thought one sunny, almost windless afternoon, I must do something today . . .

Then Richard woke for his two o'clock feed and she changed him and wandered outside with him to sit in a nook of the garden on a wicker chair in a patch of dappled shade. Fiona was pottering about in the kitchen, cooking up something fattening for dinner, no doubt.

'My, my,' India said to her distraught son as she unbuttoned her blouse, 'you are hungry! Now just take it slowly,' she kissed his downy head, 'or you'll get hiccups. Then you'll really be cranky!'

She seated herself more comfortably as he settled, and began to suck contentedly, and she stroked his head with the fingers of her free hand. But as that distinctive tawny hair—not that there was much of it—slid beneath her fingers, tears gathered in her eyes. For even at only three months old, it was obvious that Richard was going to be very like his father.

Will that be a comfort to me? India wondered. Or a torment? To have a living reminder of Giles? Pray God it's not . . . Not that I could ever hate you, my darling, only the memories.

A sound disturbed her and she looked up through a mist of tears to see the tall figure of a man standing a few feet away, outlined against the sun.

She gasped and clutched her blouse, and

Richard lost his grip on her nipple with a wail of despair.

'My God, India,' Giles Ballantyne said bitterly, and moved so that she could see him properly, the burning look of disbelief in his grey eyes, the murderously angry set of his jaw, 'isn't it a bit late to be prim?'

'I . . . I didn't realise it was you,' she stammered. 'The sun was in my eyes . . .'

'The sun has always been in your eyes,' he said tightly, mockingly. 'But I can't believe that even you would do this—to yourself, to me, to any child. I presume it is mine?' He closed his eyes briefly. 'Don't answer that,' he added, looking down at the now very upset infant in India's arms. 'Well?' he demanded switching his grey gaze to her flushed cheeks and stunned hazel eyes.

'I . . .'

'If you're expecting me to go away while you feed him, I'm afraid I'm going to disappoint you. I've been there myself, remember?' His eyes taunted her.

She flinched and looked away. But Giles Ballantyne's son was now sobbing in extreme distress, his little face crumpled and red, his fists waving angrily. She looked down at him and for a moment held him very close. 'Don't cry,' she whispered, guiding her nipple back into his mouth. But he was still sobbing as he started to suck again, indignant little wails. Then they subsided as he kneaded her breast with one tiny hand, and finally he was at peace again.

India looked up at last to see that Giles's face was wiped clean of emotion. 'What have you called him?' he asked into the tense silence.

'Richard. It was my father's name.'

'How old is he? Three months?'

'And a bit,' she whispered and cleared her throat. 'Fiona must have contacted you?'

'Yes. I'm only sorry she didn't see fit to give me some warning,' he commented drily.

'She didn't tell you?'

'No, just asked if I could come over. She sounded upset so I did. But when I arrived a few minutes ago, she did give me some intimation. All she said was, "There's someone in the garden you should see ... I hope to God I've done the right thing but I was afraid she was going to go away again ..." I knew then it had to be you. But I never expected this.'

'It ... was always on the cards, I guess,' India said huskily.

'Oh yes,' he drawled and she shivered because she knew he was very angry again. 'On the other hand, despite what you obviously *thought* was between us, I never expected you to put yourself through this without some support from me. What did you think I'd do if you'd come back and told me you were pregnant? Did you think I'd add it up like an accountant, in terms of stocks and shares? A child? My own child?'

'I didn't know *what* to think,' India said, and gasped at the sudden force of feeling that swept through her. 'But I always knew there was something wrong! I always knew that. I may be a fool about a lot of things but not that ...' She realised dimly that she was crying, great tearing sobs, and she tried to make herself stop because of Richard. Only to realise as she clutched him to her, that he'd fallen asleep. And that she couldn't stop crying and that Fiona was suddenly on the scene, taking the baby from her, saying angrily to Giles, 'Now look what you've done!'

Then she didn't remember much for a time. A strange voice, being in bed, searching desperately for Richard, until someone put him cautiously into her arms. 'Oh, thank God,' she heard herself saying hoarsely, holding him, crooning to him as he slept contentedly.

'. . . Post-natal depression,' she heard a strange voice saying then, 'is extremely common in one form or another . . .'

'I know, I know,' she wanted to shout. 'They warned me about it. But this is different . . . The last thing I want to do is harm my baby!'

'. . . it often manifests itself in a simple inability to cope . . .'

'If you only knew! You're right, I can't cope any more. I should never have come. I was coping marvellously until I came up here. My mother coped. I could have . . . there's got to be a reason for history to repeat itself.'

'India?'

'I want to sleep . . . don't!' she whispered convulsively, as hands descended upon Richard.

'My dear . . . India? It's me, Fiona. I'll look after him.'

'Don't lose him,' she mumbled. 'He's all I've got.'

'He's right here beside you. Look.'

India did, and saw Richard in his pram right beside the bed. She reached out a hand and gripped the side of it firmly.

She woke the next morning with an eerie feeling of

unreality, as if she'd done things and said things
she couldn't altogether account for. As if, despite
having slept God knows how long, she was still
inexpressibly weary. Then she turned her head, but
the pram was still beside her bed, and Richard still
in it.

'He slept,' she said wonderingly, with a confused
recollection of an early evening feed, then being
too tired to do anything herself but go back to
sleep. 'He slept all night through. That's the first
time he's done that.'

'Glory be,' Fiona mumbled, and India realised
she was in the twin bed of the pretty guest room.

'I'm sorry,' she said intensely, 'I don't know
what got into me yesterday.'

'I do,' Fiona replied with a yawn.

'Post-natal blues?'

'With complications,' Fiona agreed. 'Like a cup
of tea?'

'Yes but I'll get it, I'm not sick or anything.'

'You stay right where you are,' Fiona returned
severely.

When she came back she'd removed her hair
net, and brushed her hair. India took a cup of tea
from her gratefully, and winced because her
breasts were full and tight. 'Hope he doesn't sleep
too long,' she murmured.

'I shouldn't worry,' Fiona remarked, 'he's a very
good baby but I've noticed a singular determination about him concerning regular meals.
There! What did I say? He's stirring now.'

India bent over the pram and Master Richard
opened his eyes and stared fixedly at her for a
moment, then gave her a blinding smile.

India closed her eyes briefly. 'Oh God, he's so

like Giles, isn't he?' she whispered.

'Mmm ... I'm afraid we've got to talk about that, India.'

'I know,' India said helplessly and sipped her tea, then swallowed it hurriedly as Richard gave notice that he was not much in a smiling mood any longer.

'Perhaps there's only one thing I can say—what I did yesterday I believe was for the best, and I hope you'll forgive me.'

'Oh Fiona,' India said huskily, 'I do. In a way I'm only sorry now I didn't have the courage to do it myself. But you do see,' she lifted her head and stared at Fiona searchingly, 'how ... *impossible* it is?'

Fiona looked away first, with a sigh. 'I hope not,' she replied finally, 'because I must tell you, India, that Giles gave me to understand last night that he was going to assume full responsibility for you and the baby, whether you liked it or not.'

CHAPTER TEN

'GILES,' India said helplessly, 'you can't just commandeer me like this!'

They were standing in Fiona's garden, in the wintry sunshine, with the heady perfume of stocks and sweet peas wafting around them and the ocean below stretching like a blinding sheet of light to the horizon.

Giles squinted out to sea and for a moment India wished he'd exhibit some anger, like yesterday. But this morning there was an air of containment about him, an air of implacable purpose that was more frightening if anything.

She studied him in silence. He wore bleached cream denims and a sage-green pullover over a cream sports shirt. I've seen just that shade of green before, and in some connection with Giles, she thought, then caught her thoughts, but not before a tide of colour poured into her cheeks. For she'd remembered the colour of his curtains and bedspread in the house at Runaway Bay; but of course not only that . . .

'What is it?' he asked.

She twisted her hands together awkwardly. 'Nothing. I . . .'

But he interrupted her. 'Why did you come back, then? If you're so averse to being "commandeered" as you put it?'

'Giles . . . look,' she was having some difficulty with her voice, 'will you tell *me* something?'

'Yes. What?' He looked at her levelly.

'Why did you do it? I mean, sell Ballantyne's?'

He said nothing for a moment, then he spoke almost casually. 'Because I didn't particularly appreciate being cast in the role of a man who was prepared to marry only to acquire some shares.'

'But your father's company—all he worked for!' she said involuntarily, and immediately wished she hadn't as his mouth hardened into a straight line.

'Perhaps it was also my final ... tilt at my father,' he said then, barely audibly but with a flickering savagery. 'I gather it didn't cause you to change your mind, India,' he added, but dispassionately now.

'I didn't know,' she whispered.

'It got a lot of media attention. Where were you? Beyond the Black Stump?'

'In a sense ...'

'If you'd contacted your solicitor you'd have known.'

She could say nothing.

'Which upsets you more?' he said after a time.

'I don't know what you mean.'

'That I rejected your summing up of me, and Lance Kidder's, or that I sold Ballantyne's to prove it.' He looked at her enquiringly.

Oh God, she thought, turning away defensively, was I wrong? But what does it matter, he's not going to forgive me ...

'Will you answer my question now, India? Actually I've got two.' He put his hand on her shoulder and swung her round to face him. 'Why did you come? And what made you change your mind then? Tell me, India,' he insisted mercilessly.

She swallowed and was surprised to find a

stiffening within her, a sense of fortitude perhaps, that enabled her to say quietly but evenly, 'I came, Giles, because I thought it wasn't fair to either you or your son never to know about each other. That I would be doing to Richard exactly what my mother did to me. But I don't suppose you even know about that.'

'Yes, I do. My father told me.'

She looked at him in surprise.

'No, we didn't discuss you often, India,' he observed, 'but towards the end he ... explained some things to me. Well, he told me you'd have no one to turn to and why.'

'Oh.' India couldn't resist a tinge of bitterness.

'Go on,' Giles said flatly.

'I ... after Richard was born, I came to realise that deep down within me, I'd really resented not having a father—not even that so much as not *knowing* ... it's a feeling I can't even describe adequately, and while you can bury it in your subconscious as a child, it's not so easy to later. Yet there I was, I suddenly saw, preparing to do the same thing to Richard. And that the longer I left it the more ... complicated it could become. You could get married and have other children, and then he would be like I was, an embarrassment, an unwanted complication. That's why I came,' she said steadily. But her voice cracked a little then. 'I also thought we could be ... adult enough to work something out.'

'Like getting together?' he interrupted.

'I ... no.'

'Oh, I see. You were prepared to grant me visiting rights and then every second school holiday, perhaps, when he's older?'

'It . . . it can work out,' she insisted shakily.

He smiled unpleasantly. 'You're *looking* at a product of that kind of life, my dear India. It's the last thing I'd inflict on any child of mine. No, I agree with you that we should be adult about this. Adult enough,' he said deliberately, 'to admit that we made our bed and now we have to lie in it. After all you've been through, surely that's not too much to ask on behalf of your son?'

'It couldn't work,' she whispered with sudden tears streaming down her cheeks. 'How could it possibly work if you hate me now and can't . . .?'

'Who said anything about hating you, India?' he enquired drily. 'It's a long time since I've hated you. In fact I'm still incredibly attracted to you, strange as it may seem. After all, I sold Ballantyne's to prove it to you.'

'That . . . that's what I was afraid of,' she cried. 'You didn't have to . . .'

He laughed. 'What else would have done it? You tell me!'

She couldn't answer, only weep silently into her hands.

He let her cry for a couple of minutes then he put an arm around her shoulder and when she went to pull away, tightened it until she stood still. 'Listen to me now, India,' he said in a different voice. 'I'm taking you and Richard home to Runaway Bay. If you'd like, Fiona will come and stay with us for a while. She's offered to because the doctor we called in yesterday said you needed rest, companionship, that you were too thin and from the look of you, heading for a real breakdown. You needn't worry about me, I won't be placing any demands on you even when you're over this, if that's how you want it.'

'But that's . . .'

'India,' he interrupted and forced her to look up at him with his hand beneath her chin, 'I . . . oh hell, I came here this morning with the express intention of not upsetting you, and so far, without saying what I really came to say. Which is this. Don't you really think, despite all the shadows and the ghosts and God knows what else that come between us—don't you think that with our backgrounds, we of all people could give a kid a break? Isn't that why you came back? Truthfully? Because inside you're sick and tired of people who take their pleasures and then there's some unfortunate child to reap the consequences?'

'It wasn't like that!'

'It's probably very often not. But in your heart of hearts you don't understand being a product of it, do you?'

'No,' she whispered.

'Then don't you see that the least we can do is *try*?'

The one fat candle was solemnly lit, and Richard Ballantyne's eyes, which were a lighter version of his mother's, less brown but still with greeny flecks in them, went perfectly round with wonder. Despite being only one year old he was seldom lost for a word, and he said gravely after a moment, 'Hot!'

'Yes, darling,' India agreed. 'Mustn't touch.'

'What you've got to do is blow it out,' Fiona chimed in, and began to make extravagant blowing motions which so charmed her godson that he laughed delightedly, and for the rest of that day, practised blowing at anything and everything.

'I see we have a new trick,' Giles remarked that night, after saying good night to his son. He'd not been at the birthday party that afternoon, but so far as Richard was concerned so long as he saw his beloved father some time during the day he was content. 'Who taught him that?'

India, who had poured him a drink, laughed as she handed it to him and picked up his tie and jacket from where he'd discarded them over the back of a chair. 'Fiona.'

Giles, sprawled out in an armchair, twirled the glass idly. 'She's been terrific, hasn't she?'

'Yes. I asked her to stay for dinner, but she had something on.' She turned away.

'Don't go, India,' he said quietly.

'I was only going to hang these up . . .'

'And then disappear into the kitchen, I've no doubt. Sit down, have a drink with me. I'll get you one.' He stood up.

India hesitated then laid the jacket and tie back and sat down herself, a little self-consciously but unable to help herself. You'd think after being married for nearly nine months these ... self-conscious moments would have gone away, she reflected wryly, and jumped as Giles's knuckles grazed hers as he slid a glass into her hand.

'Oh, thanks,' she murmured.

He stood beside her, looking down at her sombrely for a moment or two before saying, 'I thought we might go out for dinner tonight. To—celebrate.'

'W-what?' India said uncertainly.

'Our son's first birthday—actually we have another thing to celebrate tonight. The first successful year in operation of the new company.'

'Of course, I forgot about that,' India said guiltily. 'It was . . . an odd coincidence that you and Jeff formed it the day Richard was born, wasn't it? And it's going well?' she added hastily, and bit her lip because she knew it was going well—she did know that much. With Giles's business acumen and Jeff's dedication, the new travel business they'd opened now had a string of branches throughout Queensland. Even after so short a time in business, the package holidays they offered had acquired a reputation for being well organised, well conceived and above all, value-for-money orientated. Both Giles's and Jeff's experience in the resort development business had been invaluable to them. Besides, she thought with a sigh, anything Giles touched probably did well. That was one of the reasons Ballantyne's was so sought after—for what Rod put into it and what Giles's vision had added. Only Paradise Resorts miscalculated in a sense, she mused. They got the company but not the driving force behind it.

She looked up suddenly. 'All right,' she said embarrassedly. 'Where would you like to go? And we'd have to organise a baby-sitter.'

Their gazes locked in a way they hadn't for a long time. 'You're a very accommodating wife, India,' he said drily then, 'you could say no.'

Her heart began to hammer uncomfortably, because she knew he was challenging her to step outside the guidelines of this marriage. But they were *your* guidelines, Giles, she thought with a sudden, stubborn tilt to her chin. Well, they were the only ones that we both seemed to be able to live by . . .

'I . . .' she said confusedly, 'no, I'd like to go out

for a change.' She looked away as his grey eyes
mocked her briefly.

'Then why don't you get ready and I'll ring the
baby-sitter.' He turned away, almost disinter-
estedly.

India eyed herself in her dressing-table mirror.
She'd put on a dress of rose-pink shantung with
long sleeves and a layered skirt; it was a dress she
hadn't worn for a long time, nearly two years, but
it had a timeless elegance—and no waistline so the
fact that it was a little loose about her waist and
hips wasn't noticeable. Despite everyone's efforts
in that direction, she hadn't quite regained what
she'd weighed before she'd conceived Richard.
When you stop feeding him, Fiona had said, you'll
put on weight. But I'm not really skinny, India
had protested and Fiona had agreed that she was
no longer like a bag of bones.

Yet it had become like a personal crusade to
Fiona to restore India to exactly what she had
been, obviously. But she'd stopped feeding
Richard three months ago and still those stubborn
few more pounds had not come. However, India
had found herself one ally—the eighteen year old
girl who lived next door-but-one with her parents
and was in her last year of school.

Belinda babysat Richard, mostly during the
afternoon when India did her shopping, but also
on the very odd occasions when Giles and India
went out at night. In fact all those occasions had
been to do with the new business. She'd conceived
an almost puppy-like admiration for India, not the
least for the way she'd managed to have a baby
and still have such a gorgeous figure.

'There *are* some changes,' India had said to her one day, half-laughingly, half embarrassed. 'You can't have a baby and be exactly the same, I'm afraid.'

'Then you must have been absolutely perfect before,' young Belinda had enthused in her forthright manner.

India had turned away suddenly. Yes, a perfect idiot.

Those words came back to taunt her, as they so often did, as she sat in front of her dressing-table in her rose-pink dress and contemplated spending an evening with Giles, out and on their own. But we're often on our own at home, she thought. And we . . . get by. She put a hand to her mouth as her lips trembled, wondering if he had the slightest idea what kind of torture it was for her, this marriage of separate beds, separate rooms?

I wonder if he understands that if I didn't paint and garden and cook and have Richard to look after, I'd go mad. I'm probably the most domesticated wife in Runaway Bay. My garden is superb now, my house the same, my baby . . . Only my painting has suffered, and the more I do the worse it gets but I still keep ploughing on . . .

She stared at her reflection, her thoughts ranging distractedly over the past nine months. Fiona had spent two weeks with them at the beginning, then for a month, Giles's regular cleaning lady had come in daily. But at the end of the month India had insisted on dispensing with her, because she'd divined by then that the platonic nature of their marriage was to continue even although she was quite well. She'd divined

some other things as well—that to be back in
Giles's company was to be possessed of a violent
thirst and hunger. To be possessed of the most
vivid memories that must have lain dormant
within her during the year they had spent apart, of
the way his hands had touched her once and his
lips. Of the way her body had responded so
incredibly . . .

But for the past nine months he'd gone out of
his way not to touch her, even in the normal
course of events. And she'd known why—he might
still be attracted to her as he'd said, but he
couldn't forgive her for not trusting him, for
forcing him to sell Ballantyne's to prove something
to her. And what else would have done it, India?
she often taunted herself. *You* tell me . . .

'Is it any wonder that the attraction has turned
bitter and is slowly dying?' she whispered to her
image in the mirror. 'Only it's not dying for me,
that's the problem. I even get depressed sometimes
when I see him with Richard, because Richard gets
so much more than I do. Not just that impersonal
kindness, he gets the real Giles, the one I knew so
briefly on Hamilton Island and for one night in
this very house . . .'

She reached for her brush and stroked it
through her hair to steady herself. Her hazel eyes
were suspiciously bright, but her thoughts would
not let up. He was going on a trip up north
tomorrow, she knew. In fact he'd spent probably
half of the last nine months away on business,
which for India was part pain, part pleasure in
roughly equal measures. It meant she could drop
her guard, but it also meant sleepless nights
wondering what he was doing, and that most

tormenting thought—was he sleeping with someone?

She had a whole gallery of women at her disposal, that she could summon to mind at will. Women she'd been scornful of once. All beautiful or fascinating ... And she sometimes couldn't believe the stabs of jealousy she felt, like sword thrusts through her heart. In fact she often thought that if any one had told her that she would become a creature of such deeply felt, violent emotions, she would never had believed them.

'Nor would I have believed how good I'd become at covering up what I felt,' she murmured and put the brush down as she heard Giles go through to his bedroom. 'But can it last for ever? Or is that what life is about? Some day you learn to live with these things, the pain goes away and even the memories fade.'

He took her to Eliza's in the heart of Surfers' and he must have booked a table because although it looked full, the captain led them to a table after only a murmured word with Giles. Perhaps he comes here often for lunch, India thought as she followed the captain. With a lady?

Then, just as they were about to be seated, a voice from the past rang out—unmistakably Brad Mortimer's. India tensed, then forced herself to turn round. And it was like history repeating itself, only Brad was with a different girl.

'Isn't it crazy how we keep meeting in restaurants!' he said enthusiastically to India, as arrangements were being made to seat them at a table for four. 'Now let me introduce you, this is

Sylvia . . .' he paused as they all seated themselves. 'And these are Giles and India Ballantyne, Sylvie, and before you go putting two and two together, India is Giles's step-mother, she was married to his father. We met on Hamilton Island, that's when I was going with Petula—she's married now, did you know? Did I say something wrong?' His voiced wound down as India stood up jerkily.

'No. I . . . I'm sorry, I'm not feeling very well,' India stammered. 'Please excuse me . . .'

Giles caught up with her in Cavill Mall. He took her hand and swung her round to face him. 'Where do you think you're going?' he demanded harshly.

'I don't know, anywhere. I don't *care!*'

Nor did she care, it seemed, that people were streaming about them on the brightly lit cobblestones, giving them strange glances as were some of the people sitting at the outdoor cafés. Because she was crying openly and trying to free herself.

'Stop it, India,' he said in a low, fierce voice and his grip on her hand threatened to crush her bones.

She swallowed and closed her eyes, and then all the fight went out of her as suddenly as it had come. Her shoulders slumped and she said in a flat, husky voice, 'If you'd like to go back, I could get a taxi home. But I can't go back.'

'If you think I particularly want to,' he said drily, 'you're mistaken.' And with her hand still in his he started to walk and after a brief hesitation she followed obediently, her head down, her hair swinging about her face.

It was small and folksy and dark and smoky, the little restaurant he finally led her into, in Orchid

Avenue. He ordered her a brandy and a Scotch for himself, and after a brief look at the short menu, two steaks.

Giles said nothing until the steaks were placed in front of them together with chips and a colourful salad, and India took a deep breath and picked up her knife and fork. Not that she felt like eating, and that must have been obvious because he said then, 'Go on, it looks good.'

It was surprisingly good, yet she didn't finish it. But he didn't comment when she pushed her plate away, and although she didn't know it, some colour had come back into her cheeks and her eyes were no longer bleak and terrified. Just blank.

He said at last, 'I gather your distress tonight is an indication of your dissatisfaction with our marriage. If we were to go home and go to bed together, would that solve anything for you?'

India had been looking down at her glass and her lashes flew up, only to veil her eyes almost immediately again.

'Would it solve anything for you?' she asked very quietly, then drained the last drop of her brandy. 'Or don't you have a problem to be solved?' she queried barely audibly. 'I'm sorry if I've been so transparent tonight, it must have been the thought of trying to explain to Brad that I was actually married to you now. Brad's got a sense of humour, hasn't he? He'd have seen the funny side of it. I remember he thought it was vastly amusing . . .'

'Stop it, India,' he cut in sharply. 'Just answer the question.'

'The really funny thing is, Giles, I can't. I don't know if it would solve anything for me, or make things worse. For instance, I've no idea if you're asking me this with a view to ... to giving me another baby. Now, practically, that's not a bad idea. It would be good for Richard and it would really cement our marriage,' she said with irony. 'Only what is there to cement?'

'India, we agreed ...'

'I'm sorry,' she said at last with a catch in her voice. 'This isn't helping much is it? I guess—it might be the answer if we're to keep ... going forward.'

Belinda was surprised to see them home so early. 'Thought you were going to make a real night of it,' she said.

'India didn't feel quite up to it,' Giles replied abruptly and added, 'I'll walk you home.'

'Oh, you don't need to worry, it's only two doors away and I don't suppose there are any mad murderers or rapists out there.' She gathered up her books.

'All the same I'd prefer to, Belinda. Here, I'll give you a hand with those. My God,' he said with a grin, 'anyone would think you were studying to be a doctor and lawyer at the same time!'

'That's what it feels like,' Belinda agreed darkly, but her sunny smile reappeared as she kissed India good night and and she could be heard chattering gaily as they walked down the path.

India stepped quietly into Richard's room and saw by the passage light that he was fast asleep with his lashes fanning like silky crescents on his cheek. She pulled the coverlet over him and resisted the sudden urge she had to gather him closely up into her arms.

She turned away reluctantly and wandered into her bedroom and began to undress, thinking that Giles was taking his time. She stood in the middle of the room in her white Viyella nightgown trimmed at the neck and wrists with fine lace, then reached for her garnet-coloured velvet robe and tied it around her waist. She hesitated, then walked back towards the lounge.

He was standing in the middle of the lounge with a glass in his hand, staring straight in front of him but he turned as she made an involuntary sound. 'I ... I didn't hear you come in,' she said nervously.

He lifted an eyebrow and set his glass down on the copper-topped table. 'As Belinda said, it's not far to go.'

The silence stretched painfully. India fiddled with her sash then they both spoke together.

'Giles . . .'

'India . . .'

He shrugged. 'You go first.'

Her lips quivered. 'I can't,' she whispered, and turned away to hide the sudden tears in her eyes.

'If,' he said with an effort, 'it's that difficult for you . . .'

She licked the salty tears on her upper lip. 'It's not,' she confessed brokenly, at last. 'You don't understand—I thought you'd *never* ask, and even now, that you don't really want it.'

He crossed the stretch of rug between them in a couple of strides and hauled her round to face him with brutal fingers digging into her upper arms. 'Say that again!' he commanded, his eyes blazing with something she couldn't put a name to.

But she could only stare up at him helplessly,

hopelessly. 'India,' he said through his teeth, 'if that's how you felt you only had to give one sign of it and I'd have ... oh God! Why didn't you?'

'I couldn't,' she wept. 'I knew it was my ... punishment for not trusting you, for forcing you to do what you did. How *could* I?' Her eyes were pleading and desperate. 'The stupid thing, the crazy thing was that if anyone should have believed you can fall in love with someone overnight, I should have, because it *happened* to me. Only ... only ...' She stopped then went on thickly, 'I was too much of a fool to see it.'

Giles closed his eyes briefly and for a fleeting, marvellous moment she thought he was going to hold her close. But it was as if he did battle with himself, and finally he put her away from him gently but decisively, and her marvellous moment died and in its place there was a feeling of dread.

'India,' he looked down for a long moment, then directly into her eyes. 'I've lied to you in a sense.' He spoke in a low but perfectly even voice. 'By omission. You were right to question this business of falling in love overnight from my point of view, because I didn't.'

It was as if all the feeling drained out of her other than a sensation of being cold, so cold ...

'I've wanted to tell you this before,' he went on, 'but I found it impossible—especially after what you once said to me. India!' His voice sharpened with concern. 'Are you all right? Don't faint on me again.'

'No,' she said hastily, and glanced round unseeingly and decided she better sit down. As she did so she heard herself saying, not because it mattered, but only to prove to herself that she was still alive, 'W-what was that that I said?'

He hesitated, watching her carefully, his dark grey eyes curiously tormented and shadowed. 'You said it was the one thing you respected me for.'

She licked her lips, not understanding and not really caring. 'Did I say that? Why? I don't seem to remember . . .'

'Yes, you did. We were talking about how people had treated you while you were married to my father, especially men.'

Her eyes widened in the pallor of her face, as recollection suddenly flooded her . . . of a rainy dusk beside the water at Paradise Point, of saying something about respecting him for having genuinely hated her, for never having . . .

'Giles?' she whispered uncertainly.

He stood in front of her with the lamplight picking up the red glints in his tawny hair, his eyes hooded and sombre, but the bearing of his tall body straight—as of someone about to confess his sins and accept the consequences.

'The truth of the matter is that from the moment I laid eyes on you, in your pretty white dress with those flowers in your hair, standing there looking a little lost at your wedding reception, I . . . wanted you as I'd never wanted anyone before.'

Her lips parted on a soundless gasp.

'Yes,' he agreed grimly, 'I must confess I found it hard to believe too. A basic, primeval lust that sprang up out of nothing—I didn't know you, I *couldn't* like you after about one minute of assessing how much younger you were than my father, not to mention the fact that an unknown girl, however beautiful she was, had put me in the position of . . . coveting my *father's* wife. So it's fair to say, India, that I started out wanting you and hating you, and hating myself for wanting you in a purely physical way.'

Her lips parted, and her eyes were shocked and stunned.

'It doesn't make pleasant hearing, does it? I knew it wouldn't,' he murmured. 'But since I've started, let me go on. They say confession is good for the soul.' His mouth twisted mockingly. 'So, I waited for it to go away, and tried to hasten its passing in a time-honoured way,' his eyes glinted sardonically, 'and I thought it *has* to, there's no rational basis for it. I'd quite convinced myself that you were nothing but a gorgeous tramp who had married for money. But it didn't go away—if anything it got worse in a rather curious way. I began to doubt my tramp theory, you didn't act like one and, even to my perverted mind, you were obviously very, very happy. So was he. It began to dawn on me then that you were the one woman I could love. Of course I refused to believe it—I used to push all those doubts away even when I told myself I should go away, that surely it would have been better than to stay and watch you so obviously happy with my father, so bereft when he died.' He closed his eyes briefly.

'Then . . . it wasn't true that you told me about being jealous? I mean . . .' She stopped.

'Oh, that was true,' he said drily. 'It was an incredibly small part of the truth, though. But I used that as a prop for a while, with a sense of righteous wrath. The only constant thing through four years of torment, and then another year of a different kind of torment, was my utter determination that no one should ever know how I felt. Never know,' his voice was suddenly flat and weary, 'how successfully I was doing it.

'Then,' he went on in that same tired voice, 'my father died, and in the midst of my grief and despair that I should have let anyone come between us, I detected, incredibly, a spark of hope. I actually found myself thinking, *it's my turn now with India*. If you can imagine,' his face was suddenly drawn and very pale, 'how I hated myself for that?'

'Oh, Giles,' she breathed, but he wouldn't let her go on. 'There's more,' he said curtly.

'Don't,' she begged.

'I have to. I decided then ... I told myself, enough of this. It's borne you enough bitterness as it is. Forget about her and anyway, it could never work. Which I tried to do very diligently, but the only way it seemed to work was to keep on treating you as I always had. Then I bought that painting. Of course I'd never seen the chair, but when I realised you had painted it, I thought, oh God, she's so lonely, so lost ... just as Dad said she would be.'

India made a small husky sound in her throat.

'That made me angry again because I knew it was *him* you were ... so lost without. Can you understand thsat?'

Their eyes locked, his burning with self-contempt, hers still supremely dazed.

'And I carried that anger to the last board meeting you attended, India,' he said after a while. 'I thought if this thing hadn't finally loosened its grip on me, I'd bludgeon it to death that day.'

'Oh God,' she whispered, and tried to stand up,

only to crumple to her knees.

'India,' he sank down beside her and took her into his arms, 'please, hear me out.'

'I don't want to, I can't bear it.'

'You don't know what I'm going to say.'

'I do,' she wept. 'That you succeeded and then this take-over bid cropped up!'

'*No*. From the minute you walked into my office I never gave that bloody take-over bid a second thought that day. Because after you'd left, I knew that none of the weapons I'd used were ever going to work. That I couldn't keep attacking you with words simply because I so much wanted to do the opposite. I'd been in love with you for a long time and *nothing* I did would ever change it. And that I had to at least try and make you ... love me in return. At least I had to *try*.'

India lifted her head, her face flushed and tear-streaked, her fingers clutching at his shirt sleeves, and a dawning of yearning hope in her eyes.

'That take-over bid,' Giles said in a low voice laced with pain, 'was only ever an ironic coincidence. All the same, it gave me a chance, I thought, to prove to you that I loved you. But when you came back you hadn't even known about it. The only reason you'd come back was because of Richard. And the supreme irony, so I reasoned, was that you were far more concerned that I should have let my father's life work go, than *why* I had. In fact, I thought it upset you so much, you were poised to go again without even seeing me. Only I found I couldn't let you go, even if he was still there between us. But I did make one resolution—not to touch you or ... anything, unless you seemed to want it.'

'If only you'd told me all this before,' she said, her throat working, her lips unsteady.

'Would you have understood?' he asked, his eyes searching hers. 'Or would you have felt that I was no better than Lance Kidder, and felt contaminated, and that it was another, much deadlier thrust at what you'd had with my father?'

'Giles,' she whispered, 'I don't know. But I do know this—I've come a long way since the night we talked about these things in your car. What you've told me finally makes sense of things, and that's all that matters to me now. The one thing I didn't want to hear just now, and was terrified that I would, was that you don't love me. No,' she put a finger to his lips, 'let me finish, I have some explaining to do too. I know now that what I felt for your father and what I feel for you overlap in some ways but never can in others. I *was* a child then, not in years but in most other ways but with you I'm finally a woman, an equal. And that I love you under any circumstances. I suppose Rob started my initiation, but only you could have completed it.

'I saw myself as a creature of divided loyalties or worse, faithless. Now I see that you can love people in different ways and while I'll always love your father's memory and what he did for me, it was only a stage along the road. If he'd lived I might never have come to see or understand any of this, and it's futile anyway to speculate on it; in fact, I haven't for a long time. His memory is at peace within me at last.'

They were sitting awkwardly on their heels, very close but quite unaware of any discomfort.

'Do you really mean that?' he said at last.

'I do.' India spoke as if it was a vow. 'And,' she went on, in the same low, husky but steady voice, 'what really upset me about you selling Ballantyne's was not on his account, but because I knew how much it meant to *you* on his account. All I could think was that I'd run away again, and forced you into doing it because I was a coward and too stupid, not worthy of it . . .' Her voice cracked and she buried her head in his shoulder.

'Oh God, don't,' he said softly, and having some difficulty with his own voice. 'All that matters is that we've finally . . . got there. Don't cry, my love, my dearest love . . .'

Two days later, Giles, who should have been in North Queensland but wasn't, said to India, 'Has it occurred to you that we missed out on a honeymoon?'

'No,' India admitted honestly, and added demurely, 'it's only very recently occurred to me that I'm really and truly married to you.'

Giles stretched beside her and took her into his arms. 'And what's the verdict?' he asked gravely.

'Well,' she considered, 'it does strange things to one, being really married. For instance, here we are at half-past four in the afternoon, in bed. And what's more we quite shamelessly got Belinda to take Richard out for a while in order so to be. I can perceive that I've taken to living a double life. On the other hand . . .' She stopped dramatically.

'Go on,' he said casually, but with his fingers roving her bare body, stroking the silky inner skin of her thighs.

'I can't—not while you're doing that,' she whispered.

'I'll stop, then.'

'No, that would be worse.' She kissed his naked shoulder lingeringly.

'But I'm determined to hear more about this double life.'

'I love it,' she said tremulously.

'And I'm quite hopelessly, passionately addicted to it and you,' he murmured, touching her breasts lightly but possessively. 'Did you know you're even more beautiful than you were?'

'No. I don't see how . . . I mean . . .'

'You'll have to take my word for it, then, but you are. I—I'd have given years of my life to see you pregnant with Richard, India.'

'But . . .'

'I guess it's a very male instinct,' he said wryly. 'It was also a little hard not to be jealous—not that I minded his infatuation with these,' he cupped her breasts, 'only that I was excluded.'

'I used to get miserable too,' she said raggedly. 'I mean I was happy for him but every time you picked him up I felt left out.'

'It's a miracle he's turned out so well with such a crazy father.'

'And mother. Giles, what I said about another baby the other night, I know it sounded . . . well . . . but deep down I meant it.'

'For Richard's sake?'

'No, mine,' she confessed in a low shaken voice, 'and yours. To be able to go through it again as it should be done.'

He held her so hard that she could barely breathe.

Later, when she was lying drowsily beside him with hardly the energy to move, he said, 'Talking of honeymoons, I had a thought. Not quite your conventional honeymoon but . . . India?' He sat up and bent over her.

'Go on, I'm listening,' she murmured, and smiled a secret, dreamy little smile of perfect fulfilment.

He grinned and kissed her tenderly. 'I *love* you.' She clung to him.

'Well,' he continued eventually, 'I thought we could retrace our steps in a way. You know the island you never got to see?' She nodded after a moment. 'I kept the lease as part of the deal with Paradise Resorts. They were more interested in the northern New South Wales—Southern Queensland region anyway. And I've since built a house up there.'

'Just *a* house?' Her eyes were wide.

'Mmm. For us, I never quite gave up hope . . . It's nothing grand, more of a holiday home, a tropical hideaway with only generator power at the moment and rather primitive plumbing. But I thought of going up there for a week or so and taking Fiona with us, and Belinda—the school holidays are coming up. Then I thought we could spend a few days on Hamilton to round it off.'

India closed her eyes.

'Would you enjoy that, my darling?' he asked huskily.

'Oh, Giles,' she whispered, picturing the beautiful Whitsundays, the magic of an uninhabited island, and the magic Hamilton would always hold for her, 'yes.'

'Good,' he said promptly. 'I'll start to make the arrangements.'

'But—I mean, I'd *love* Fiona and Belinda to

come but if it's to help out with Richard, I don't
need two people.'

'Well,' he pursued with a perfectly wicked glint
in his eye, 'I thought they could keep each other
company when we were doing this.' His grey gaze
roamed her body meaningfully.

'You have a very devious mind, Giles,' she said
with her lips twitching.

'I know,' he agreed. 'On the other hand, we
would spend some time with them. We could take
them to the Reef . . . no,' he said softly. 'I'm not
that devious. They've been great and it would be
good to repay them like that, wouldn't it?'

'It would be super.'

'Talking of whom,' he said with an effort,
'Belinda and Richard anyway, they'll be back
soon.'

'Oh!' India's hand flew to her mouth and she
tried to sit up. 'How could I have forgotten?' she
said guiltily.

He looked at her and laughed.

'Oh, *you*,' she said with mock severity. 'Don't
think it's always going to be like this! One fine day
I'll have my way with you so that you won't have
the energy to move or even want to, let alone
think!'

'I can't wait,' he murmured, his eyes gleaming
with laughter. 'How about tonight?'

'You don't believe me, do you?' she said darkly,
and went to get up.

'On the contrary, I have the greatest faith in
you, India,' he replied gravely, easily resisting all
her efforts to leave the bed.

'Giles, no,' she whispered, going pink as he
started to kiss her breasts. 'Belinda is quite likely

to waltz in here to find out what's going on! Please let me go,' she begged.

'I can see we'll have to train Belinda in certain things if she's to come away with us—I loved the way you said please like that,' he murmured. 'One more time ought to do it . . .'

'Oh, I always knew you were impossible, Giles Ballantyne,' she moaned breathlessly. *'Please . . .'*

'Done,' he said promptly, and lifted his head. But the teasing laughter in his eyes softened to something so tender that it almost took her breath away. 'But you stay here and relax,' he reassured, and kissed her lips gently. 'I'll deal with Belinda and bring Richard into you. Love me?'

'Crazy about you,' she answered with her heart in her eyes. 'For ever and ever.'

Coming Next Month

959 THE CALL OF HOME Melinda Cross
After her father's death and her mother's recovery from her breakdown,
an American painter returns to her childhood haunt to heal her own
wounds—and comes up against a man who's as much in need of love as
she is.

960 WOMAN OF HONOUR Emma Darcy
Labeled a home-wrecker when a certain lawyer's brother-in-law neglected
to mention his marriage, an Australian chef turns workaholic. But guess
who her next Dial-A-Dinner Party client is?

961 TRY TO REMEMBER Vanessa James
A distraught amnesiac and a forceful merchant banker search from
Devon to Morroco for something to jolt her memory. But what really
knocks her for a loop is her feelings for him.

962 A MAN POSSESSED Penny Jordan
Fate brings an old friend of a widow's late husband back into her life, the
man who'd rejected her in the midst of her bleak marriage. But it seems
he'd desired her, after all.

963 PASSIONATE VENGEANCE Margaret Mayo
A London designer finds herself fired on trumped-up charges. Her
reputation's smeared. So the job at Warrender's Shoes seems like a
lifeline—until she discovers her boss's motives in hiring her.

964 BACHELOR IN PARADISE Elizabeth Oldfield
The soap opera star a British author interviews in Florida isn't the vain
celebrity she'd expected. He lives frugally, disappears every Wednesday,
declares parts of his life "off-limits"—and fascinates her to no end!

965 THE ARRANGEMENT Betsy Page
Marry the woman from Maine or forfeit control of the family business,
an uppercrust Bostonian warns his son. But the prospective bride is as
appalled by the arrangement as the groom—so they have one thing in
common, at least.

966 LOVE IN THE MOONLIGHT Lilian Peake
A young journalist wants to warn her sister in Cornwall that the man
she's dallying with is a heartbreaker. But how can she—when she's still in
love with the man herself?

Available in March wherever paperback books are sold, or through
Harlequin Reader Service:

In the U.S.
P.O. Box 1397
Buffalo, N.Y.
14240-1397

In Canada
P.O. Box 603
Fort Erie, Ontario
L2A 5X3

Take 4 best-selling love stories FREE
Plus get a FREE surprise gift!

Six exciting series for you every month... from Harlequin

Harlequin Romance·
The series that started it all

Tender, captivating and heartwarming...
love stories that sweep you off to faraway places
and delight you with the magic of love.

◆

Harlequin Presents·
Powerful contemporary love stories...as individual as the women who read them

The No. 1 romance series...
exciting love stories for you, the woman of today...
a rare blend of passion and dramatic realism.

◆

Harlequin Superromance®
It's more than romance... it's Harlequin Superromance

A sophisticated, contemporary romance-fiction
series, providing you with a longer,
more involving read...a richer mix of complex plots,
realism and adventure.